CONTENTS

Section Four: Supernatural

Section Five: The Individual

Section Six: Mini-Sagas

UNWIN HYMAN SHORT STORIES

SHORTIES

(19)

**INCLUDING
FOLLOW ON
ACTIVITIES**

EDITED BY ROY BLATCHFORD

Unwin Hyman English Series

Series editor: Roy Blatchford
Advisers: Jane Leggett and Gervase Phinn

Unwin Hyman Short Stories
Openings   edited by Roy Blatchford
Round Two   edited by Roy Blatchford
School's OK   edited by Josie Karavasil and Roy Blatchford
Stepping Out   edited by Jane Leggett
That'll Be The Day   edited by Roy Blatchford
Sweet and Sour   edited by Gervase Phinn
It's Now or Never   edited by Jane Leggett and Roy Blatchford
Pigs is Pigs   edited by Trevor Millum
Dreams and Resolutions   edited by Roy Blatchford
Shorties   edited by Roy Blatchford
First Class   edited by Michael Bennett
Snakes and Ladders   edited by Hamish Robertson
Crying For Happiness   edited by Jane Leggett
Funnybones   edited by Trevor Millum

Unwin Hyman Collections
Free As I Know   edited by Beverley Naidoo
Solid Ground   edited by Jane Leggett and Sue Libovitch
In Our Image   edited by Andrew Goodwyn
Northern Lights   edited by Leslie Wheeler

Unwin Hyman Plays
Stage Write   edited by Gervase Phinn
Right on Cue   edited by Gervase Phinn
Scriptz   edited by Ian Lumsden

Published in 1989 by
Unwin Hyman Limited
15/17 Broadwick Street
London W1V 1FP
Selection and notes © Roy Blatchford 1989

British Library Cataloguing in Publication Data
Blatchford, Roy
    Shorties: including follow on activities.—
    (Unwin Hyman short stories)
    I. Title
    823'.01'08   [FS]

    ISBN 0–04–448041–5

Typeset by TJB Photosetting Ltd., Grantham, Lincolnshire
Printed in Great Britain by Billing & Sons Ltd., Worcester
Series cover design by Iain Lanyon. Cover illustration by Paul Dickinson

Introduction

The aim of this collection is to provide a resource for students moving towards GCSE English and English Literature, and Standard Grade English, though much of the material will appeal across the secondary age range. The stories have been selected first and foremost because they are fine examples of the short story genre, and are perhaps best enjoyed when read aloud and shared with a group of students. They also offer opportunities to talk and write about issues that are of concern and relevance to young people.

A special dimension of *Shorties* — as the title highlights — is its concentration on *short* short stories, in the firm belief that for so many students *accessibility* is the key to getting going on the reading path, and to subsequent enjoyment and understanding. Increasingly teachers find that the short story genre is particularly valuable for classroom use right across the age and ability range. At the same time it is important to stress that the very brevity of some of these tales in no way indicates a diminished literary merit.

The craft of Stephen Leacock, James Plunkett, Olive Schreiner, Kate Chopin, Patricia Miles and others gathered here serves only to reinforce V S Pritchett's proper claim:

'The short story is the most *memorable* form of fiction. It is memorable because it has to tell and ring in every line. It has to be as exact as a sonnet or a ballad. It is, in essence, 'poetic' in its impulse'.

Where better to begin a literature course — at whatever level — than contrasting these stories with ballads, sonnets and the opening pages of great novels?

'How do I get students started with their own writing?' — a familiar cry amongst English teachers! One of the explicit purposes of *Shorties* is to offer just such a resource, whether in the shape of the intriguing crime portraits 'Bird Talk' and 'The Old Flame', or through the unnerving futuristic visions of Asimov and Henry Sleasar. The 'new genre' of the Mini-Sagas is guaranteed to encourage even the most reluctant of young writers.

For teachers interested in working along thematic lines the volume has been further organised to cater for that need. Equally, for those wishing to study authors' styles and techniques it is quite possible to dip into the various sections. For individual students engaged in Wider Reading or Open Study assignments, the Humour, Crime, Science Fiction, Supernatural and The Individual categories should provide a convenient guide.

The 'Follow On' activities offer a range of approaches to help students of *all* abilities, whether in building up a coursework folder or in preparing for essays written under timed examination conditions. They aim to encourage students to:
— work independently and collaboratively
— consider the short story as a genre; language and style of a writer; structure and development of plot; development of character; setting.
— examine the writer's viewpoint and intentions
— respond critically and imaginatively to the stories, orally and in writing
— read a variety of texts, including quite difficult ones
— read more widely

One important footnote: the activities are divided under three broad headings:

Before Reading	— enabling the student to anticipate and speculate about what is going to happen.
During Reading	— building up a picture of what is going on and what may happen next, interacting with the text as the 'engaged' reader.
After Reading and *Extended*	— allowing time to reflect on the setting, events, characters, issues and themes within the stories; giving opportunities for discussion, and for personal, critical and discursive writing.

Teachers are therefore recommended to preview the 'Follow On' section before reading the stories with students.

By way of lead-in to the collection perhaps it is worth recalling master storyteller Sean O'Faolain's dictum:

'The short-story writer's problem of language is the need for a speech which combines suggestion with compression... If I have to choose one word to describe short-story language I would either say that it is engrossed, or that it is alert'.

Having already read these stories in the classroom, I foresee that your own students will be both engrossed and alert!

Roy Blatchford

STEPHEN LEACOCK

H̲o̲ for Happiness

'Why is it,' said someone in conversation the other day, 'that all the really good short stories seem to contain so much sadness and suffering and to turn so much on crime and wickedness? Why can't they be happy all the time?'

No one present was able to answer the question. But I thought it over afterwards, and I think I see why it is so. A happy story, after all, would make pretty dull reading. It may be all right in real life to have everything come along just right, with happiness and good luck all the time, but in fiction it would never do.

Stop, let me illustrate the idea. Let us make up a story which is happy all the time and contrast it as it goes along with the way things happen in the really good stories.

Harold Herald never forgot the bright October morning when the mysterious letter, which was to alter his whole life, arrived at his downtown office.

His stenographer brought it in to him and laid it on his desk.

'A letter for you,' she said. Then she kissed him and went out again.

Harold sat for some time with the letter in front of him. Should he open it? After all, why not?

He opened the letter. Then the idea occurred to him to read it. 'I might as well,' he thought.

'Dear Mr Herald' (so ran the letter), 'if you will have the kindness to call at this office, we shall be happy to tell you something to your great advantage.'

The letter was signed John Scribman. The paper on which it was written bore the heading 'Scribman, Scribman & Company, Barristers, Solicitors, etc, No. 13 Yonge St.'

A few moments later saw Harold on his way to the lawyers' office. Never had the streets looked brighter and more cheer-

1

ful than in this perfect October sunshine. In fact, they never had been.

Nor did Harold's heart misgive him and a sudden suspicion enter his mind as Mr Scribman, the senior partner, rose from his chair to greet him. Not at all. Mr Scribman was a pleasant, middle-aged man whose countenance behind his gold spectacles beamed with good-will and good-nature.

'Ah, Mr Harold Herald,' he said, 'or perhaps you will let me call you simply Harold. I didn't like to give you too much news in one short letter. The fact is that our firm has been entrusted to deliver to you a legacy, or rather a gift...Stop, stop!' continued the lawyer, as Harold was about to interrupt with questions, '...our client's one request was that his name would not be divulged. He thought it would be so much nicer for you just to have the money and not know who gave it to you.'

Harold murmured his assent.

Mr Scribman pushed a bell.

'Mr Harold Herald's money, if you please,' he said.

A beautiful stenographer wearing an American Beauty rose at her waist entered the room carrying a silken bag.

'There is half a million dollars here in five-hundred-dollar bills,' said the lawyer. 'At least, we didn't count them, but that is what our client said. Did you take any?' he asked the stenographer.

'I took out a few last night to go to the theatre with,' admitted the girl with a pretty blush.

'Monkey!' said Mr Scribman. 'But that's all right. Don't bother with a receipt, Harold. Come along with me: my daughter is waiting for us down below in the car to take us to lunch.'

Harold thought he had never seen a more beautiful girl than Alicia Scribman. In fact he hadn't. The luxurious motor, the faultless chauffeur, the presence of the girl beside him and the bag of currency under the seat, the sunlit streets filled with happy people with the bright feeling of just going back to work, full of lunch — the sight of all this made Harold feel as if life were indeed a pleasant thing.

'After all,' he mused, 'how little is needed for our happiness!

2

Half a million dollars, a motor-car, a beautiful girl, youth, health — surely one can be content with that...'

It was after lunch at the beautiful country home of the Scribmans that Harold found himself alone for a few minutes with Miss Scribman.

He rose, walked over to her and took her hand, kneeling on one knee and pulling up his pants so as not to make a crease in them.

'Alicia!' he said. 'Ever since I first saw you, I have loved you. I want to ask you if you will marry me?'

'Oh, Harold,' said Alicia, leaning forward and putting both her arms about his neck with one ear against the upper right-hand end of his cheekbone. 'Oh, Harold!'

'I can, as you know,' continued Harold, 'easily support you.'

'Oh, that's all right,' said Alicia. 'As a matter of fact, I have much more than that of my own, to be paid over to me when I marry.'

'Then you will marry me?' said Harold rapturously.

'Yes, indeed,' said Alicia, 'and it happens so fortunately just now, as papa himself is engaged to marry again and so I shall be glad to have a new home of my own. Papa is marrying a charming girl, but she is so much younger than he is that perhaps she would not want a grown-up stepdaughter.'

Harold made his way back to the city in a tumult of happiness. Only for a moment was his delirium of joy brought to a temporary standstill.

As he returned to his own apartment, he suddenly remembered that he was engaged to be married to his cousin Winnie...The thing had been entirely washed out of his mind by the flood-tide of his joy.

He seized the telephone.

'Winnie,' he said, 'I am so terribly sorry. I want to ask you to release me from our engagement. I want to marry someone else.'

'That's all right, Hal!' came back Winnie's voice cheerfully. 'As a matter of fact, I want to do the same thing myself. I got engaged last week to the most charming man in the world, a

3

little older, in fact quite a bit older than I am, but ever so nice. He is a wealthy lawyer and his name is Walter Scribman...'

The double wedding took place two weeks later, the church being smothered with chrysanthemums and the clergyman buried under Canadian currency. Harold and Alicia built a beautiful country home at the other side — the farthest-away side — of the city from the Scribmans'. A year or so after their marriage, they had a beautiful boy, and then another, then a couple of girls (twins), and then they lost count.

There. Pretty dull reading it makes. And yet, I don't know. There's something about it, too. In the real stories Mr Scribman would have been a crook, and Harold would have either murdered Winnie or been accused of it, and the stenographer with the rose would have stolen the money instead of just taking it, and it wouldn't have happened in bright, clear October weather but in dirty old November — oh no, let us have romance and happiness, after all. It may not be true, but it's better.

A Violent Tale

'Yes,' said the violinist, 'and what's more I could tame any animal you care to mention, in exactly the same way.'

'Right, you're on,' said a man leaning against the bar. 'I'll bet you a thousand pounds you can't do it with my three lions.'

'Done,' said the violinist, and off everybody trooped to the near-by circus where this other bloke was a lion-tamer.

The violinist took up a position in the centre of the cage, and started to play a slow, haunting melody. 'Right,' he called, 'let the first one in.'

With a blood-curdling roar, the first lion sprang into the ring and made straight for the musician, then stopped in its tracks, assumed a dreamy expression, sank to the floor, put its head on its front paws, and listened entranced.

'Now let the second one in,' called the violinist, continuing to play.

Exactly the same happened as with the first lion. The two of them exchanged soulful glances, obviously deeply moved by the music.

Then the violinist called for the remaining lion to be let in. This one bounded into the cage, paused for a moment to survey the scene, then made straight for the violinist, who was still playing so beautifully, and ate him up.

The other two lions went up to the third one, looking very annoyed. 'What's the idea, doing that when we were listening to that wonderful music?'

The third lion put a fore-paw up to his ear and said, 'Eh?'

SAKI

The Reticence of Lady Anne

Egbert came into the large, dimly lit drawing-room with the air of a man who is not certain whether he is entering a dovecote or a bomb factory, and is prepared for either eventuality. The little domestic quarrel over the luncheon-table had not been fought to a definite finish, and the question was how far Lady Anne was in a mood to renew or forgo hostilities. Her pose in the arm-chair by the tea-table was rather elaborately rigid; in the gloom of a December afternoon Egbert's pince-nez did not materially help him to discern the expression of her face.

By way of breaking whatever ice might be floating on the surface he made a remark about a dim religious light. He or Lady Anne were accustomed to make that remark between 4.30 and 6 on winter and late autumn evenings; it was a part of their married life. There was no recognised rejoinder to it, and Lady Anne made none.

Don Tarquinio lay astretch on the Persian rug, basking in the firelight with superb indifference to the possible ill-humour of Lady Anne. His pedigree was as flawlessly Persian as the rug, and his ruff was coming into the glory of its second winter. The page-boy, who had Renaissance tendencies, had christened him Don Tarquinio. Left to themselves, Egbert and Lady Anne would unfailingly have called him Fluff, but they were not obstinate.

Egbert poured himself out some tea. As the silence gave no sign of breaking on Lady Anne's initiative, he braced himself for another Yermak effort.

'My remark at lunch had a purely academic application,' he announced; 'you seem to put an unnecessarily personal significance into it.'

Lady Anne maintained her defensive barrier of silence. The bullfinch lazily filled in the interval with an air from *Iphigénie en Tauride*. Egbert recognised it immediately, because it was the only air the bullfinch whistled, and he had come to them

6

with the reputation for whistling it. Both Egbert and Lady Anne would have preferred something from *The Yeomen of the Guard*, which was their favourite opera. In matters artistic they had a similarity of taste. They leaned towards the honest and explicit in art, a picture, for instance, that told its own story, with generous assistance from its title. A riderless warhorse with harness in obvious disarray, staggering into a courtyard full of pale swooning women, and marginally noted 'Bad News,' suggested to their minds a distinct interpretation of some military catastrophe. They could see what it was meant to convey, and explain it to friends of duller intelligence.

The silence continued. As a rule Lady Anne's displeasure became articulate and markedly voluble after four minutes of introductory muteness. Egbert seized the milk-jug and poured some of its contents into Don Tarquinio's saucer; as the saucer was already full to the brim an unsightly overflow was the result. Don Tarquinio looked on with a surprised interest that evanesced into elaborate unconsciousness when he was appealed to by Egbert to come and drink up some of the spilt matter. Don Tarquinio was prepared to play many rôles in life, but a vacuum carpet-cleaner was not one of them.

'Don't you think we're being rather foolish?' said Egbert cheerfully.

If Lady Anne thought so she didn't say so.

'I daresay the fault has been partly on my side,' continued Egbert, with evaporating cheerfulness. 'After all, I'm only human, you know. You seem to forget that I'm only human.'

He insisted on the point, as if there had been unfounded suggestions that he was built on Satyr lines, with goat continuations where the human left off.

The bullfinch recommenced its air from *Iphigénie en Tauride*. Egbert began to feel depressed. Lady Anne was not drinking her tea. Perhaps she was feeling unwell. But when Lady Anne felt unwell she was not wont to be reticent on the subject. 'No one knows what I suffer from indigestion' was one of her favourite statements; but the lack of knowledge can only have been caused by defective listening; the amount of information available on the subject would have supplied material for a monograph.

Evidently Lady Anne was not feeling unwell.

Egbert began to think he was being unreasonably dealt with; naturally he began to make concessions.

'I daresay,' he observed, taking as central a position on the hearth-rug as Don Tarquinio could be persuaded to concede him, 'I may have been to blame. I am willing, if I can thereby restore things to a happier standpoint, to undertake to lead a better life.'

He wondered vaguely how it would be possible. Temptations came to him, in middle age, tentatively and without insistence, like a neglected butcher-boy who asks for a Christmas box in February for no more hopeful reason than that he didn't get one in December. He had no more idea of succumbing to them than he had of purchasing the fish-knives and fur boas that ladies are impelled to sacrifice through the medium of advertisement columns during twelve months of the year. Still, there was something impressive in this unasked-for renunciation of possibly latent enormities.

Lady Anne showed no sign of being impressed.

Egbert looked at her nervously through his glasses. To get the worst of an argument with her was no new experience. To get the worst of a monologue was a humiliating novelty.

'I shall go and dress for dinner,' he announced in a voice into which he intended some shade of sternness to creep.

At the door a final access of weakness impelled him to make a further appeal.

'Aren't we being very silly?'

'A fool,' was Don Tarquinio's mental comment as the door closed on Egbert's retreat. Then he lifted his velvet forepaws in the air and leapt lightly on to a bookshelf immediately under the bullfinch's cage. It was the first time he had seemed to notice the bird's existence, but he was carrying out a long-formed theory of action with the precision of mature deliberation. The bullfinch, who had fancied himself something of a despot, depressed himself of a sudden into a third of his normal displacement; then he fell to a helpless wing-beating and shrill cheeping. He had cost twenty-seven shillings without the cage, but Lady Anne made no sign of interfering. She had been dead for two hours.

Baby X

Once upon a time a baby named X was born. This baby was named X so that nobody could tell whether it was a boy or a girl. Its parents could tell of course but they couldn't tell anybody else. They couldn't even tell Baby X at first.

You see, it was all part of a very important, secret scientific Xperiment known officially as Project Baby X.

Long before Baby X was born a lot of scientists had to be paid to work out the details of the Xperiment and to write the Official Instructions Manual for Baby X's parents and most important of all to find the right set of parents to bring up Baby X.

But finally the scientists found the Joneses, who really wanted to raise an X more than any other kind of baby, no matter how much trouble it would be. Ms and Mr Jones had to promise that they would take equal turns caring for X and feeding it and singing it lullabies.

The day the Joneses brought their baby home lots of friends and relatives came over to see it. None of them knew about the secret Xperiment though. When the Joneses smiled and said, 'It's an X,' nobody knew what to say. They couldn't say 'Look at her cute little dimples' and they couldn't say 'Look how strong his muscles are' and they couldn't say just plain 'kitchy coo'. In fact they all thought the Joneses were playing some kind of rude joke.

But of course, the Joneses were not joking. 'It's an X' was absolutely all they would say, and that made the friends and relatives very angry. The relatives all felt very embarrassed about having an X in the family. 'People will think there's something wrong with it' some of them whispered. 'There is something wrong with it,' others whispered back.

'Nonsense' the Joneses told them cheerfully. 'What could possibly be wrong with this perfectly adorable X? Nobody could answer that except Baby X who had just finished its bottle. Boaby X's answer was a loud satisfied burp!

Clearly, nothing at all was wrong. Nevertheless none of the relatives felt comfortable about buying a present for a Baby X. The cousins who sent the baby a tiny pair of boxing gloves would not come and visit anymore, and the neighbours who sent a pink flowered romper suit drew their curtains when the Joneses passed their house.

Ms and Mr Jones had to be Xtra careful about how they played with little X. They knew that if they kept bouncing it in the air and saying how strong and active it was they'd be treating it more like a boy than an X. But if all they did was cuddle and kiss it and tell it how sweet and dainty it was, they'd be treating it more like a girl than an X. On page 1654 of the Official Instructions Manual the scientists prescribed 'plenty of bouncing and plenty of cuddling both'. X ought to be strong and sweet and active—forget about the dainty altogether.

Meanwhile the Joneses were worrying about other problems. Toys, for instance. And clothes. Mr Jones wandered helplessly up and down the aisles finding out what X needed. But everything in the store was piled up in sections marked 'Boys' or 'Girls'. There were 'Boy's pyjamas' and 'Girl's underwear' and 'Boy's fire engines' and 'Girl's housekeeping sets.' Mr Jones went home without buying anything for X. That night, he and Ms Jones consulted page 2326 of the Official Instructions Manual. 'Buy plenty of everything' it said firmly. So they bought plenty of sturdy blue pyjamas in the Boys department and cheerful flowered underwear in the Girls department and they bought all kinds of toys. A boy doll that made pee-pee and cried Papa, and a girl doll that talked in three languages and said 'I am the president of General Motors'. They also bought a story book about a brave princess who rescued a handsome prince from his ivory tower and another one about a sister and brother who grew up to be a baseball star and a ballet star and you had to guess which was which.

By the time X grew big enough to play with other children the Joneses' trouble had grown bigger too. Once a little girl grabbed X's shovel in the sandbox and zonked X on the head with it. 'Now Tracy', the little girl's mother scolded. 'Little girls mustn't hit little…' and she turned to ask X, 'Are you a boy or a girl dear?' Mr Jones who was sitting near held his breath. X smiled and even though its head had never been zonked so hard before, replied 'I'm an X'. 'You're a what?' exclaimed the lady. 'You're a little brat, you mean.' 'But little girls mustn't hit little X's either,' said X retrieving the shovel and smiling again. 'What good does hitting do anyway?' X's father grinned at X. At their next secret Project X meeting the scientists grinned and said Baby X was doing fine.

But it was then time for X to start school. The Joneses were really worried about this because school was even more full of rules for boys and girls, and there were no rules for X's. The teacher would tell boys to form one line and girls to form another. There would be boys' games and girls' games and boys' secrets and girls' secrets. The school library would have a list of recommended books for boys and another for girls. Pretty soon boys and girls would hardly talk to each other. What would happen to poor little X?

The Joneses had asked X's teacher if the class could line up alphabetically instead of boys and girls, and if X could use the principal's bathroom as it wasn't marked Boy or Girl. X's teacher promised to take care of all these problems; but no one could help with X's biggest problem, 'Other Children'.

After school X wanted to play with Other Children. 'How about football?' it asked the girls. They giggled. 'How about weaving baskets?' it asked the boys. They giggled too and made faces. That night Ms and Mr Jones asked how things had gone at school. X said sadly the lessons were OK but otherwise school was a terrible place for an X—it seemed as if Other Children never wanted an X for a friend.

Once more, the Joneses read the Official Instructions Manual. Under 'Other Children' they found the message 'What do you expect? Other Children have to obey all the silly boy and girl rules because their parents taught them to. Lucky X, you don't have to stick to rules at all. All you do is be yourself. PS We're not saying it will be easy.'

X liked being itself. But X cried a lot that night partly because it felt afraid. So X's father held X tight and cuddled it and couldn't help crying too. And X's Mother cheered them both up by reading an Xciting story about an enchanted prince called Sleeping Handsome who woke up when Princess Charming kissed him. The next morning they all felt much better and little X went back to school with a brave smile.

There was a relay race in the gym, and a baking contest and X won the relay race and almost won the baking contest Xcept it forgot to light the oven, which only proves that nobody is perfect.

One of the Other Children noticed something else. 'Winning or losing doesn't seem to matter to X. X seems to have fun at boy and girl skills.'

'Come to think of it' said another child, 'Maybe X is having twice the fun we are.' So after school that day, the girl who won the baking contest gave X a big slice of cake and the boy who nearly won the race asked X to race him home. From then on some funny things happened. Susie, who sat next to X, refused to wear pink dresses to school anymore. She wanted to wear red and white check overalls like X's, they were better for climbing monkey bars. Then Jim, the class football nut, started wheeling his sister's doll's pram round the football field. He'd put on his football uniform except the helmet. Then he put the helmet in the pram lovingly tucked under a set of shoulder pads. Then he'd push it round the football field singing 'Rockabye baby' to his helmet. He told his family X did the same thing so it must be OK, after all, X was now the team's quarterback.

Susie's parents were horrified by her behaviour and Jim's were worried sick about him. But the worst came when the twins Joe and Peggy decided to share everything with each other. Peggy used Joe's hockey skates and his microscope and shared his newspaper round. Joe used Peggy's needlework kit and cookbooks and took three of her baby-sitting jobs. Peggy used the lawnmower and Joe the vacuum cleaner.

Their parents weren't one bit pleased with Peggy's wonderful chemistry experiments or with Joe's embroidered pillows. They didn't care that Peggy mowed the lawn better and that Joe vacuumed the carpet better. In fact they were furious. 'It's all that little X's fault' they agreed. 'Just because X doesn't know what it is, or what it's supposed to be, it wants to get everyone mixed up too.' Peggy and Joe were forbidden to play with X. So was Susie and then Jim and then all the Other Children. But it was too late. The Other Children stayed mixed up and happy and free and refused to go back to the way they had been before.

Finally Joe and Peggy's parents decided to call an emergency meeting of the Parent Teacher Association, in order to discuss the X problem. They sent a report to the principal saying X was a disruptive influence. They wanted immediate action. The Joneses, they said, should be forced to tell whether X was a boy or a girl, and then X should be forced to behave like whichever it was. If the Joneses refused to say, the Parent Teacher Association said X must have an Xamination. The school doctor should examine X and issue a report.

At exactly 9 o'clock the next day X reported to the school surgery. The principal, the Parent Teacher Association, teachers, classmates and Ms and Mr Jones waited outside. Nobody knew the details of the test X was to be given but everybody knew it would be very hard and that it would reveal exactly what everyone wanted to know about X but were afraid to ask.

At last the door opened. Everyone crowded round to hear the results. X didn't look any different; in fact X smiled. But the doctor looked terrible as if he was crying. 'What happened?' everyone shouted. Had X done something disgraceful? 'Wouldn't be surprised' said Peggy and Joe's parents. 'Did X flunk the whole test?' cried Susie's parents. 'Or just most of it?' yelled Jim's parents.

'Oh dear', sighed Ms and Mr Jones. 'Sssh' said the principal, 'the doctor is trying to speak'. Wiping his eyes and clearing his throat, the doctor began in a hoarse whisper. 'In my opinion' he whispered 'in my opinion young X here...is just about the least mixed up child I have ever examined'. 'Hooray for X,' yelled one of the children. The Other Children clapped and cheered. 'Sssh' said the principal, but no one did.

Later that day X's friends put on their overalls and went to see X. They found X in the yard playing with a very tiny baby that none of them had seen before. The baby was wearing very

tiny red and white overalls. 'How do you like our new baby?'
X asked the Other Children proudly.

'It's got cute dimples,' said Jim.

It's got strong muscles too,' said Susie.

'What kind of baby is it?' asked Joe and Peggy.

X frowned at them 'Can't you tell?' Then X broke out into a
big mischievous smile. 'It's a Y!!'

ANTON CHEKHOV

The Objet d'Art

Holding under his arm an object carefully wrapped up in No.223 of the *Stock Exchange Gazette*, Sasha Smirnoff (an only son) pulled a long face and walked into Doctor Florinsky's consulting-room.

'Ah, my young friend!' the doctor greeted him. 'And how are we today? Everything well, I trust?'

Sasha blinked his eyes, pressed his hand to his heart and said in a voice trembling with emotion:

'Mum sends her regards, Doctor, and told me to thank you...I'm a mother's only son and you saved my life—cured me of a dangerous illness...and Mum and me simply don't know how to thank you.'

'Nonsense, lad,' interrupted the doctor, simpering with delight. 'Anyone else would have done the same in my place.'

'I'm a mother's only son...We're poor folk, Mum and me, and of course we can't pay you for your services...and we feel very bad about it, Doctor, but all the same, we—Mum and me, that is, her one and only—we do beg you most earnestly to accept as a token of our gratitude this...this object here, which...It's a very valuable antique bronze—an exceptional work of art.'

'No, really,' said the doctor, frowning, 'I couldn't possibly.'

'Yes, yes, you simply must accept it!' Sasha mumbled away as he unwrapped the parcel. 'If you refuse, we'll be offended, Mum and me...It's a very fine piece...an antique bronze...It came to us when Dad died and we've kept it as a precious memento...Dad used to buy up antique bronzes and sell them to collectors...Now Mum and me are running the business...'

Sasha finished unwrapping the object and placed it triumphantly on the table. It was a small, finely modelled old bronze candelabrum. On its pedestal two female figures were standing in a state of nature and in poses that I am neither bold

15

nor hot-blooded enough to describe. The figures were smiling coquettishly, and altogether seemed to suggest that but for the need to go on supporting the candlestick, they would leap off the pedestal and turn the room into a scene of such wild debauch that the mere thought of it, gentle reader, would bring a blush to your cheek.

After glancing at the present, the doctor slowly scratched the back of his ear, cleared his throat and blew his nose uncertainly.

'Yes, it's a beautiful object all right,' he mumbled, 'but, well, how shall I put it?...You couldn't say it was exactly tasteful...I mean, décolleté's one thing, but this is really going too far...'

'How do you mean, going too far?'

'The Arch-Tempter himself couldn't have thought up anything more vile. Why, if I were to put a fandangle like that on the table, I'd feel I was polluting the whole house!'

'What a strange view of art you have, Doctor!' said Sasha, sounding hurt. 'Why, this is a work of inspiration! Look at all that beauty and elegance—doesn't it fill you with awe and bring a lump to your throat? You forget all about worldly things when you contemplate beauty like that...Why, look at the movement there, Doctor, look at all the air and *expression*!'

'I appreciate that only too well, my friend,' interrupted the doctor, 'but you're forgetting, I'm a family man—think of my small children running about, think of the ladies.'

'Of course, if you're going to look at it through the eyes of the masses,' said Sasha, 'then of course this highly artistic creation does appear in a different light...But you must raise yourself above the masses, Doctor, especially as Mum and me'll be deeply offended if you refuse. I'm a mother's only son —you saved my life...We're giving you our most treasured possession...and my only regret is that we don't have another one to make the pair...'

'Thank you, dear boy, I'm very grateful...Give Mum my regards, but just put yourself in my place—think of the children running about, think of the ladies...Oh, all right then, let it stay! I can see I'm not going to convince you.'

'There's nothing to convince me of,' Sasha replied joyfully. 'You must stand the candelabrum here, next to this vase. What a pity there isn't the pair! What a pity! Goodbye, then, Doctor!'

When Sasha had left, the doctor spent a long time gazing at the candelabrum, scratching the back of his ear and pondering.

'It's a superb thing, no two ways about that,' he thought, 'and it's a shame to let it go...But there's no question of keeping it here...Hmm, quite a problem! Who can I give it to or unload it on?'

After lengthy consideration he thought of his good friend Harkin the solicitor, to whom he was indebted for professional services.

'Yes, that's the answer,' the doctor decided. 'As a friend it's awkward for him to accept money from me, but if I make him a present of this object, that'll be very *comme il faut*. Yes, I'll take this diabolical creation round to him—after all, he's a bachelor, doesn't take life seriously...'

Without further ado, the doctor put on his coat, picked up the candelabrum and set off for Harkin's.

'Greetings!' he said, finding the solicitor at home. 'I've come to thank you, old man, for all that help you gave me—I know you don't like taking money, but perhaps you'd be willing to accept this little trifle...here you are, my dear chap—it's really rather special!'

When he saw the little trifle, the solicitor went into transports of delight.

'Oh, my word, yes!' he roared. 'How do they think such things up? Superb! Entrancing! Wherever did you get hold of such a gem?'

Having exhausted his expressions of delight, the solicitor glanced round nervously at the door and said:

'Only be a good chap and take it back, will you? I can't accept it...'

'Why ever not?' said the doctor in alarm.

'Obvious reasons...Think of my mother coming in, think of my clients...And how could I look the servants in the face?'

'No, no, no, don't you dare refuse!' said the doctor, waving his arms at him. 'You're being a boor! This is a work of inspiration—look at the movement there...the *expression*...Any more fuss and I shall be offended!'

17

'If only it was daubed over or had some fig leaves stuck on...'

But the doctor waved his arms at him even more vigorously, nipped smartly out of the apartment and returned home, highly pleased that he'd managed to get the present off his hands...

When his friend had gone, Harkin studied the candelabrum closely, kept touching it all over, and like the doctor, racked his brains for a long time wondering what was to be done with it.

'It's a fine piece of work,' he reflected, 'and it'd be a shame to let it go, but keeping it here would be most improper. The best thing would be to give it to someone...Yes, I know—there's a benefit performance tonight for Shashkin, the comic actor. I'll take the candelabrum round to him as a present—after all, the old rascal loves that kind of thing...'

No sooner said than done. That evening the candelabrum, painstakingly wrapped, was presented to the comic actor Shashkin. The whole evening the actor's dressing-room was besieged by male visitors coming to admire the present; all evening the dressing-room was filled with a hubbub of rapturous exclamations and laughter like the whinnying of a horse. Whenever one of the actresses knocked on the door and asked if she could come in, the actor's husky voice would immediately reply:

'Not just now, darling, I'm changing.'

After the show the actor hunched his shoulders, threw up his hands in perplexity and said:

'Where the hell can I put this obscenity? After all, I live in a private apartment—think of the actresses who come to see me! It's not like a photograph, you can't shove it into a desk drawer!'

'Why not sell it, sir?' advised the wig-maker who was helping him off with his costume. 'There's an old woman in this area who buys up bronzes like that...Just ask for Mrs Smirnoff—everyone knows her.'

The comic actor took his advice...

Two days later Doctor Florinsky was sitting in his consulting-room with one finger pressed to his forehead, and was thinking about the acids of the bile. Suddenly the door flew open and in rushed Sasha Smirnoff. He was smiling, beaming, and his whole figure radiated happiness...In his hands he was holding something wrapped up in newspaper.

'Doctor!' he began, gasping for breath. 'I'm so delighted! You won't believe your luck—we've managed to find another candelabrum to make your pair!...Mum's thrilled to bits...I'm a mother's only son—you saved my life...'

And Sasha, all aquiver with gratitude, placed the candelabrum in front of the doctor. The doctor's mouth dropped, he tried to say something but nothing came out: he was speechless.

STEPHEN LEACOCK

The Conjurer's Revenge

'Now, ladies and gentlemen,' said the conjurer, 'having shown you that the cloth is absolutely empty, I will proceed to take from it a bowl of goldfish. Presto!'

All around the hall people were saying, 'Oh, how wonderful! How does he do it?'

But the Quick Man on the front seat said in a big whisper to the people near him, He—had—it—up—his—sleeve.'

Then the people nodded brightly at the Quick Man and said, 'Oh, of course', and everybody whispered round the hall, 'He—had—it—up—his—sleeve.'

'My next trick,' said the conjurer, 'is the famous Hindustani rings. You will notice that the rings are apparently separate; at a blow they all join (clang, clang, clang) — Presto!'

There was a general buzz of stupefaction till the Quick Man was heard to whisper, 'He—must—have—had—another—lot—up—his—sleeve.'

Again everybody nodded and whispered, 'The—rings—were—up—his—sleeve.'

The brow of the conjurer was clouded with a gathering frown.

'I will now,' he continued, 'show you a most amusing trick by which I am enabled to take any number of eggs from a hat. Will some gentleman kindly lend me his hat? Ah, thank you—Presto!'

He extracted seventeen eggs, and for thirty-five seconds the audience began to think that he was wonderful. Then the Quick Man whispered along the front bench, 'He—has—a—hen—up—his—sleeve,' and all the people whispered it on. 'He—has—a—lot—of—hens—up—his—sleeve.'

The egg trick was ruined.

It went on like that all through. It transpired from the whispers of the Quick Man that the conjurer must have concealed up his sleeve, in addition to the rings, hens, and fish, several packs of cards, a loaf of bread, a doll's cradle, a live guinea-pig, a fifty-cent piece, and a rocking-chair.

The reputation of the conjurer was rapidly sinking below zero. At the close of the evening he rallied for a final effort.

'Ladies and gentlemen,' he said, 'I will present to you, in conclusion, the famous Japanese trick recently invented by the natives of Tipperary. Will you, sir,' he continued, turning toward the Quick Man, 'will you kindly hand me your gold watch?'

It was passed to him.

'Have I your permission to put it into this mortar and pound it to pieces?' he asked savagely.

The Quick Man nodded and smiled.

The conjurer threw the watch into the mortar and grasped a sledge hammer from the table. There was a sound of violent smashing, 'He's—slipped—it—up—his—sleeve,' whispered the Quick Man.

'Now, sir,' continued the conjurer, 'will you allow me to take your handkerchief and punch holes in it? Thank you. You see, ladies and gentlemen, there is no deception; the holes are visible to the eye.'

The face of the Quick Man beamed. This time the real mystery of the thing fascinated him.

'And now, sir, will you kindly pass me your silk hat and allow me to dance on it? Thank you.'

The conjurer made a few rapid passes with his feet and exhibited the hat crushed beyond recognition.

'And will you now, sir, take off your celluloid collar and permit me to burn it in the candle? Thank you, sir. And will you allow me to smash your spectacles for you with my hammer? Thank you.'

By this time the features of the Quick Man were assuming a puzzled expression. 'This thing beats me,' he whispered, 'I don't see through it a bit.'

There was a great hush upon the audience. Then the conjurer drew himself up to his full height and, with a withering look at the Quick Man, he concluded:

'Ladies and gentlemen, you will observe that I have, with

this gentleman's permission, broken his watch, burnt his collar, smashed his spectacles, and danced on his hat. If he will give me the further permission to paint green stripes on his overcoat, or to tie his suspenders in a knot, I shall be delighted to entertain you. If not, the performance is at an end.'

And amid a glorious burst of music from the orchestra the curtain fell, and the audience dispersed, convinced that there are some tricks, at any rate, that are not done up the conjurer's sleeve.

It's Slower by Lift

'Mallow and Marsh?' echoed the hall-porter. 'They're on the fourth floor. There's a self-operating lift opposite or you can walk. You'd do better to walk.'

'Four floors!' I said.

'That lift's tricky,' he replied.

'I'm used to lifts,' I said, and prodded the calling-button.

The lift appeared at once. I smiled at the hall-porter—not patronisingly, but as if to imply that in my opinion a child could operate so simple a mechanism. But when I turned to enter the lift I found it had already departed.

'It's gone,' said the hall-porter. 'You wasn't quick enough.' This was hard to deny, so I said nothing and called the lift again.

The hall-porter sang among his letters. 'Keep your finger on the button,' he said gaily, 'or you'll be here all day.' I pushed my finger fiercely into the wall and held it there.

The lift arrived after some minutes, and this time I stepped inside without delay. I pressed the fourth-floor button. The lift shuddered uncertainly and then began a palsied descent to the basement. Through the ground-floor window I caught sight of the hall-porter slowly shaking his head.

We lurched to a standstill. Before I could reach the controls the doors opened and seven sturdy men and a wheelbarrow of cement entered with a rush. I was engulfed and pinned against a side wall. The man next to me put his lips to my ear and shouted 'Where you going, guv?'

He's going up,' said a voice.

We stopped at the ground floor, and the man in charge of the wheelbarrow shouted 'All out!' As the people behind me started to press forward I said 'I don't want the ground floor.' The next moment I was carried through the doors and into the hall. By the time I returned the lift had gone.

'I see you're back again,' said the hall-porter.

'Yes,' I said shortly.

'You're dead-set on riding up?'

'Dead-set,' I answered.

'Well, I suppose I'd better help.' His whole demeanour became brisk and masterful. 'Listen!' he commanded, putting his ear to the door. 'It's stopped at the third. Ah! Timms' voice. He's the upstairs messenger and he's taking the tea to the fourth.' The ancient machinery rumbled.

'Caught him!' he said, and the lift stopped. 'You see,' he added in kindly explanation, 'you can break the circuit by pulling down the door handle. Now to bring him down.' He pressed the calling-button.

'Bring him down?' I said. 'Couldn't we wait until he has finished his journey?'

'It saves time this way,' the hall-porter pointed out.

'But do you mean he can't do anything about it?' I asked.

'He's got his hands full. Tray. He can't do a thing.'

I was impressed by the hall-porter's grasp of the situation, but I still felt uneasy. 'Do you think he'll mind?' I said.

'Mind!' he said. 'He'll be fuming.'

We heard Timms' voice long before the lift arrived. There was no doubt that the unexpected change in the direction of the lift had annoyed him.

The hall-porter opened the doors. 'Going up?' he inquired. Timms rushed out.

'You just wait until I put this tray down,' he shouted. We moved speedily into the lift.

'Very poor sort,' observed the hall-porter. 'He always carries on alarming when I do this to him. Can't stand a joke.' At that moment the lift stopped with a jolt and started to move downwards.

'That's Timms,' announced the hall-porter. 'Watch the correct counter-move.' He pressed the emergency stop, then the fourth-floor button. The lift ascended once again. The next ten minutes were devoted to move and counter-move, and the lift changed direction seventeen times. I was a little dazed, or I might have appreciated more fully the skill and cunning of both players. At the end of it Timms appeared to have tired. I was breathless. The hall-porter was triumphant.

'His tea's getting cold,' he said. 'I thought for a minute it was going to be stalemate.'

'What next?' I asked.

'No need to worry now,' said the hall-porter, 'we're almost clear of the third already.' Just then the lift stopped again. The hall-porter flew to the controls.

'We're stuck,' he said at length. 'It won't go.' I decided to take the situation in hand myself, and rang the alarm bell.

'You've done it now,' he said. 'That'll bring the electrician up here and he'll create.'

'Create what?' I asked coldly.

'Something awful,' he replied.

The electrician was a man of slow reflexes, and half an hour passed before he sought the cause of the alarm. As he opened the door I bent down and put my face to the aperture between the bottom of the lift and the top of the doorway.

'We're stuck,' I said.

'So that's it,' he said. 'I thought for a minute the cable had broke. You'd better squeeze through and climb down on my shoulders.'

It was a difficult operation, but with the electrician dragging at my lapels and the hall-porter pushing mightily from the rear I emerged at last and tottered up the stairs. I knocked at the door of Mallow and Marsh. The secretary answered.

'I'm Clegg,' I said. 'I have an appointment—'

'I'm afraid the office is empty,' she interrupted. 'Both Mr Mallow and Mr Marsh left some time ago.'

'I got stuck in the lift,' I said.

'How odd,' she remarked—and gave me a smile, as if to indicate that in her opinion a child could operate so simple a mechanism.

A Touch of Genius

I met Danny O'Donnell in the main street of Ballyross at about eight o'clock on that winter evening. At the best of times Danny was a miserable, half-starved looking oddity who owned the skinniest, most woebegone example of an Irish terrier you ever clapped eyes on, and that evening, with a hint of snow in the air and the wind making a chimney of the narrow street, I found myself feeling sorry for him—a dangerous luxury so far as Danny is concerned, because he's the greatest toucher in Ireland, with an infallible instinct for any hint of softness in the heart of a likely client. I should explain, in case you might think me hardhearted, that everyone in Ballyross gave Danny food and clothes to try to improve him—but it never seemed to have any effect, good, bad or indifferent. Danny could eat five meals a day and still manage to look half famished.

'Where are you off to, Danny?' I asked him.

'Up to meet the bus,' he said, 'to see if I can raise the price of a pint.'

In the matter of drink Danny had made a fine art of providing for himself. He was an old soldier, with an old soldier's perpetual thirst, who drank his way through his pension two days after he drew it and it was his habit, when he was broke, to try raising a few bob by meeting the bus at the top of the main street, and singing for the passengers during the half-hour wait. He always took the dog with him, knowing of course that the woebegone spectacle of the pair of them was enough to draw tears from a glass eye. It was alright in summer, but in winter I didn't fancy his chances and I said so.

'You'll be lucky if there's anybody at all to sing to,' I said to him.'

'I'll have to take that chance,' Danny said. Then he looked at me out of the corner of his eye. 'Unless, of course, you were feeling like saving me the trouble.'

'I'll ramble up to the bus with you, Danny,' I said to him. I'd stood him three free pints that week already and that was the limit I'd laid down for myself.

When we got as far as the bus Danny let an oath out of him and when I had a look for myself I saw why. The only people in it were an elderly gentleman and a youngster of about eight —his nephew, by the looks of things. Naturally, there was no sense at all in singing to a house as poor as that.

'You're bunched, Danny,' I said.

'Don't be too sure,' said Danny and off with him into the bus.

There was a cocky note in his voice that made me hang around to see what would happen, because I'll say this for Danny, he was a resourceful man, not easily put off the trail of free drink. I saw him talking to the elderly man and after a while the nephew and the gentleman got up and left. They went off in the direction of the village, while Danny followed at a distance. It appears he'd told the old man there was half an hour to kill and that the whiskey in Tim O'Leary's was as good a cure for frozen feet as anything devised by a benevolent providence.

'And where were you thinking of going yourself, Danny?' said I.

'Down to Tim's for a pint,' said Danny, 'what else.'

He was as cocky as you please and I knew now that getting a pint had become a question of honour with him.

'And how much have you got?' said I.

'I've tuppence,' Danny admitted.

'You won't get a pint for that,' I reminded him.

'If I don't,' said Danny, 'I'll have a damn good try.'

The upshot was I followed him into Tim's myself. I expected he'd have a go at what I called the dog trick and I was right. The dog was as cute as a christian and whenever a stranger came into Tim's it used to go over, plant its skinny chin on the stranger's lap and look up at him with that adoring and trustful look that all dogs can conjure up when occasion demands it. Danny had it trained to this, of course, and he used to come over after a while and apologise at length for the dog's unmannerly behaviour. Nine times out of ten it led to a conversation and ended in the stranger asking Danny to have a drink. I fell for it myself on my first visit to Tim O'Leary's the previous summer, so I know what I'm talking about.

However, the elderly gentleman was in no mood for skinny animals. He was at the counter coaxing himself to a ball of malt and when the dog planted it chin on his knee he gave it a push with his hand that nearly dislocated its jaw. Danny called the dog to him with a great show of anger, gave it another wallop for good measure—to teach it manners, moryah, and then went over to the nephew, who was sitting at a table with the blank look on his face that all kids seem to wear when they're working their way through a packet of biscuits. I watched closely. Danny patted the nephew on the head and said in a loud voice that he was a fine little man. Then he started a rigmarole, asking what age he was, was he going to school, what book was he in—all that class of blarney, for about ten or twelve minutes. You could see the old uncle at the counter beginning to lap it up. Then Danny said the boy must have another packet of biscuits.

'How much is the biscuits?' he shouted over to Tim.

'What they always were—twopence,' Tim shouted back. You could see Danny's antics had him feeling a bit impatient.

'Throw us over a packet,' said Danny. Danny caught the biscuits and gave them to the nephew.

'A bird never flew on one wing, son,' he said, 'isn't that a fact now.' The voice would put you in mind of Daddy Christmas.

The kid lit into the biscuits right away and Danny went up to pay for them.

'You shouldn't have done that,' the old man said to him.

'Yerra—what's a packet of biscuits,' said Danny, as though not taking much interest, with such a grand wave of his hand that you'd think he was the factory that made them.

'Were you going to have a drink?' asked the old man.

'I was thinking of it,' said Danny.

'Just a moment, then,' said the old man. He rooted in his pocket, slapped a half crown on the counter and said, 'You'll have this one on me.'

Danny looked surprised.

'Indeed then and I won't,' he said, firmly.

'I insist,' the old gentleman said, and I don't think I ever saw a man so anxious for the honour of standing another man a drink. It was the packet of biscuits that had done the trick, of course, I could see that.

'What will it be?' the old man insisted.

Danny hesitated beautifully. Then, with the look of a man who is only doing it to be agreeable, he gave in.

'I'll have a pint, so,' he said.

When he was raising it to his lips he had a look over his shoulder at me, to see how I was taking it, I suppose, and I raised my glass with his.

'You're the greatest chancer in Ireland,' I told him, when the old gentleman and the nephew had left.

'I'd want to be,' said Danny with such a hard look at me that I found myself breaking my rule and buying him another.

TIMOTHY CALLENDER
An Assault on Santa Claus

When Barry first heard of Santa Claus, he was puzzled. He wanted to make sure that his grandfather had heard aright.

'You mean, you never know?' his grandfather asked. 'Santa Claus never bring nothing for you at Christmas yet?'

'No,' Barry said.

'Lord, boy, I could imagine how you does behave when you inside you parents home,' Grandfather said. 'Is only when you behave good that you can get any presents from Santa Claus.'

Barry nodded slowly.

'You must try and behave good this Christmas,' Grandfather said. 'I feel sure that if you behave good he may leave something for you when he pass through.'

'Is a whole lot of children he have to visit. You think he have enough toys for all of them?'

'Yes, man. Santa Claus always carry along the exact amount of toys.'

Barry thought about it all the Christmas season. He couldn't understand how Santa Claus would find out, but he made sure that he behaved himself. He was very obedient to all his grandfather said. Day by day he restrained himself from numerous temptations. He hoped that Santa was taking careful note of it all.

'You sure he know how good I behaving?' he asked his grandfather.

'Santa know what you deserve,' Grandfather said. 'You just wait and see if he don't bring the same carpentry set that you say you would like for Christmas.'

So Barry hoped, with the same fervour that he hoped Santa was noticing his good behaviour. All things considered, it was an easy way to gain a valuable gift.

It was a remarkable change. Grandfather was pleased. 'Why

30

you can't behave so all the while?' he asked. 'Is the first time I ever see you so quiet and obedient. I hear all about how you was behaving before, you know. Your parents tell me how much trouble you always getting yourself into. They tell me how you always fighting at school, how you always getting licks, and how you involve yuhself with the police and Probation Officer too. But look how nice you behaving now. Why you can't behave so all the while?'

'Is all them boys that does interfere with me first,' Barry muttered.

'I must tell yuh parents how well you behave all the time you spend vacation here with me.'

Barry nodded.

Christmas Eve came. Barry was in a state of suppressed excitement all day. Evening took long in coming.

'Tonight is the night,' Grandfather said at supper. 'You mustn't forget to put out something for Santa to drop presents in.'

'Is all right,' Barry said. 'I have a crocus bag tie onto the bedstead.'

Grandfather laughed. 'No, boy. You can't make it look like you expect everything. A crocus bag look too greedy. Why you don't put a ordinary paper bag?'

'All right,' Barry said. But he didn't like it much. He had begun to feel that he had behaved well long enough to deserve more than a paper bag of gifts, even if the carpentry set was one of them. Santa had a whole big bag of gifts, and plenty more where they came from. He wondered how he could outwit Santa as he hung up his paper bag. Wondered if it was possible for Santa to make a mistake and give him more than he intended.

'We'll have to leave the window open,' he told Grandfather. 'We ain't have no chimney on this house.'

'Is all right,' Grandfather answered, and laughed. 'Is obvious to me that you never hear 'bout the things Santa can do. You ain't know he could even come through the keyhole?'

'He come just like a magic-man, then,' Barry said.

'You kin say so. But remember, he ain't going come unless you fall asleep, because he really don't like no children to see him.'

'All right. I going to bed now,' Barry said.

Grandfather smiled when he left. He knew that Barry, like every other one of his grandsons, would stay awake to see Santa Claus.

Barry lay down without sleeping. His eyes were open but he was very still. He could hear his heartbeat sounding through the pillow. He heard the clock strike midnight. Santa must come sometime soon.

He had barely begun to doze when the sound of the door-lock woke him. He stiffened. From where he lay he looked directly past his feet toward the door. The door was swinging open. Barry's heart raced.

He saw the figure in the doorway; big, fat, covered in red silky clothes. The light from the street outside came through the window silhouetting him. Barry saw the huge grey bag on his shoulder, heard the clinks and knocks of many things inside the bag. Barry's heart raced. He knew he was going to attempt something no child had attempted before. He wanted the whole bag of toys.

As Santa stepped forward and bent over the paper bag at the foot of the bed, Barry reached over the side of the bed, down to the floor. He gripped his grandfather's mighty walking stick and brought it up with a grunt. He barely made out Santa's head, and he aimed and let fly. Whang! The bag flew from Santa's shoulder. Santa clapped his hands to his head and tumbled on the floor.

Barry sprang from the bed. He was halfway out of the room with Santa's bag on his shoulder when he heard his grand-father's voice: 'Lord have mercy, uh dead, uh dead!'

LEN GRAY
Little Old Lady from Cricket Creek

Art Bowen and I were trying to analyse performance evaluations when Penny Thorpe, my secretary, walked into the office.

'Yeah, Penny. What's up?'

'Mr Cummings, there's a woman out in the lobby. She's applying for the filing clerk's job.' Penny walked over and laid the application form on my desk.

'Good, good. I only hope she's not one of those high-school drop-outs we've been getting.' I stopped, staring at the form. 'Age sixty-five! What the hell are we running around here? A playground for Whistler's mother?'

Art put his Roman nose in it. 'Now, Ralph, let's take it easy. Maybe the old gal's a good worker. We can't kick 'em out of the building just because they've been around a few years. How's the application?'

Good old Art. Always the peacemaker.

'Well,' I said doubtfully, 'it says her name is Mabel Jumpstone. That's right. Jumpstone. Good experience. Seems qualified. You game for an interview?'

'Sure. Why not? Let's do one together.'

This is against the company policy of Great Riveroak Insurance Company. All personnel interviewers are to conduct separate interviews and make individual decisions—at least that's what we're supposed to do. Usually we double up and save time.

Penny remained standing in front of my desk, tapping her pencil. 'Well?' she asked haughtily, which sums up her disposition perfectly.

'OK, Penny. Send Mrs Jumpstone in.'

Mrs Jumpstone came shuffling into the office, smiling and nodding her head like an old grey mare. Her black outfit looked like pre-World War I. She had on a purple hat with pink

33

plastic flowers round the brim.

She sat down and said, 'Hello there!' Her voice was almost a bellow.

I looked at Art, who was leaning forward in his chair, his mouth open, his eyes round.

'Er . . . Mrs Jumpstone,' I began.

'Mabel. Please.'

'OK, Mabel. This is Mr Bowen, my associate.' I waved a hand at Art, who mumbled something inappropriate. 'This is a very interesting application, Mabel. It says here you were born in Cricket Creek, California.'

'That's right, young man. Home of John and Mary Jackson.' She smiled at me, proud of the information.

Art bent over, scratching his wrist. 'John and Mary Jackson?'

'Oh, yes,' she replied, 'the gladiolus-growers.'

He tried to smile. I'll give him credit. 'The—the—oh, yes, of course. It must have slipped my mind. Let me see that application, Ralph.' He grabbed it from the desk and took a few minutes to study it thoroughly.

Mabel and I sat and watched each other. Every once in a while she'd wink. I tried looking at the ceiling.

Art glanced up and snapped, 'You worked at Upstate California Insurance for ten years. Why did you quit?' Sharp-thinking Art. He made a career of trying to catch people off guard. I'd never seen him do it yet.

Mabel shrugged her tiny shoulders. 'Young man, have you ever lived up North? It's another world. Cold and foggy. I just had to leave. I told Harry—that's my husband, who passed away recently, God rest his soul—that we had to come down here. Mr Bowen, you wouldn't believe how much I enjoy the sun. Of course, you've never been in Cricket Creek,' she added, which was true, of course. I doubted very much if Art had even heard of Cricket Creek.

Art looked as if he wanted to hide. Mabel smiled brightly at him, nodding her head pleasantly.

'Mabel,' I said, 'the job we have open entails keeping our personnel files up to date. Quite a bit of work, you know, in an office this size.'

'Really?'

'Really. It even requires a bit of typing. You *can* type?'

'Oh, heavens, yes. Would you like me to take a test?'

'Er . . . yes, that might be a good idea. Let's go and find a typewriter. Coming, Art?'

He grinned. 'Wouldn't miss it for the world.'

We walked out of the office. Art whispered in my ear, 'About ten words a minute would be my guess.'

It turned out to be more like ninety: I handed Mabel one of our surveys on employee retention and told her to have a go at it. She handled the typewriter like a machine-gun. The carriage kept clicking back and forth so fast that Art almost got a sore neck watching the keys fly.

Our applicant handed me three pages. I couldn't find a single error. Art looked over each page as if he were examining the paper for fingerprints. He finally gave up, shaking his head.

Mabel went back to my office. Art and I walked over to a corner, Art holding the typed sheets.

'Well, what do you think?' he asked.

'She's the best typist in the building. Definitely. Without a doubt.'

She's different. But you're right. Check her references.'

'And if they're OK?'

He shrugged. 'Let's hire ourselves a little old lady from Cricket Creek.'

Art poked his head in my door the next day. 'What about our typewriter whiz?'

'I just called her to offer her the job. Application checked out perfectly.'

He laughed. 'I bet she raises a few eyebrows.'

In fact, within two months Mabel Jumpstone was the most popular employee in the building. Whenever someone had a birthday she brought in a cake and served it during the afternoon break. And people with problems started coming to her. She arrived early each morning and stayed late. She never missed a day off work. Not one.

Six months after we hired her, Art walked slowly into my office. His eyes were glassy and his mouth was slack. He slumped down heavily in a chair.

'What's the matter with you?' I asked.

'The cash mail,' he groaned.

We receive quite a lot of cash from our customers. Once a week, on Friday, we take it to the bank. It was Friday.

'What about the cash mail, Art? Come on, what's the matter?'

He looked at me, blinking. 'Harvey was taking it to the bank. He called ten minutes ago. He was robbed. Conked. Knocked out. And guess who did it?'

'Who?'

'Mabel. Mabel Jumpstone. Our little old lady.'

'You're kidding. You've got to be *kidding*, Art.'

He shook his head. 'Harvey said she wanted a lift to the bank. After they got going, she took a pistol out of her handbag and told him to pull over. Harvey said it looked like a cannon. The gun, I mean. He's just woken up. The money and Harvey's car are gone. So's Mabel.'

I stared at him, 'I can't believe it!'

'It's true. Every word. What are we going to do?'

I snapped my fingers. 'The application! Come on.'

We ran to the filing cabinets and opened the one labelled 'Employees'. The application was gone, of course. There was a single sheet inside the manila folder. It was typed very neatly. '*I resign. Sincerely yours, Mabel.*' The name had been typed, too. There was no handwritten signature. Mabel had never written anything. She always insisted on everything being typed.

Art stared at me. 'Do you remember anything on the application? Anything? The references?' He was pleading.

'For Pete's sake, Art, it was six months ago!' I paused for a moment. 'I can remember *one* thing. Just one.'

'What?'

'She came from Cricket Creek. I wonder if there *is* a Cricket Creek?'

We checked.

There wasn't.

I finally got home to my two-bedroom bachelor apartment late that evening. The police had been sympathetic. Real nice to us. They didn't even laugh when we told them they were after a little old lady of sixty-five. They asked for a photograph or a sample of handwriting.

We didn't have either.

I opened a can of beer and then walked into one of the bedrooms.

Mabel was sitting on the bed, neatly counting $78,000 into two separate piles.

I looked at her, smiled, and said, 'Hi, Mom.'

GLENDA ADAMS

R*econstruction of an Event*

It is a Tuesday morning. The doorbell wakes her up. She may
have heard the footsteps on the concrete path leading to the
front door just a second or two before the bell rang. The sun is
high enough to light up the lime-green umbrellas and
lollipop-pink houses printed on her curtains. The jacaranda
tree outside her bedroom window casts a shadow on the wall.
She has overslept.

Does it matter that it is the shadow of a jacaranda? Rather
than dwell on the shadows and the type of tree casting them,
just state what time it is. No scene setting, no exposition.

It is Tuesday morning. The doorbell wakes her up. She has
overslept. It is nine o'clock. There is no sound in the house. No
footsteps. She guesses that everyone has gone to work and forgotten her. The doorbell rings. She intends to get up and
answer it, but instead decides to spend the day, and possibly
all days thereafter, in bed sleeping. She closes her eyes and
begins the drift back to sleep. The doorbell rings. She sits up
with difficulty. Good manners prevail. It is rude not to answer
and one spends years learning not to be rude.

It is not plausible, never to have been rude. Also, she has to
get up sooner or later, so why not answer the door? Why this
repeating of the doorbell rings, the doorbells rings? Also, her
thoughts and wishes are irrelevant and throw no light on the
matter. It is necessary to state only what happens. No opinions.

The doorbell rings. It is nine o'clock. Tuesday morning. She
came in the night before, expecting them to be waiting up for
her. All was quiet, and she was grateful. The father normally
lies awake whenever she goes out at night. He longs to sleep.
Then, after she comes home, he tosses and turns and grunts
and growls in bed and finally gets up to walk around the
house and let it be known that he has had no sleep and that

38

nothing has gone unnoticed. The next day he gives a speech to the effect that the daughter is giving him grey hairs and driving him to an untimely grave. He often composes his epitaph, beginning 'They will rue the day' and ending 'and they will all be sorry when I'm gone.' The whole thing has become a laughing matter, a family joke.

No background. None of the above is necessary or necessarily true. Just what happens.

She goes out, comes home late, and goes to bed. The doorbell rings. It is nine o'clock the next morning. Tuesday. She stands up then she falls right over. She lies on the floor. It feels pleasant enough. She can stay right where she is on the floor and continue sleeping. The doorbell rings again. She crawls to the door, hauling her dressing gown around her. She uses the door jamb to hoist herself up. In the hallway are her mother and her brother. They are steadying themselves against the walls. The smell of gas is everywhere. 'Is it an earthquake?' she inquires. The brother starts laughing, staggering away from the wall, then back again to continue leaning against it. She has never heard him laugh so much. 'In case of earthquake, stay in the doorway. Safest place,' the brother says, laughing and laughing.

Not credible. They all think that there is an earthquake just because they are a bit dizzy and have to lean against walls? Simply not possible in this part of the world where there are no earthquakes. But if they believe there is an earthquake, why does the brother laugh? An earthquake is a serious business. Don't they smell the smell? Don't they immediately know that something is wrong? Do they really stagger and sway like that?

The doorbell rings. The mother, the brother and the daughter get up to answer it. They arrive in the hallway at the same time. The mother feels her way along the walls to the front door and opens it. She has an arm through one sleeve of her dressing gown. The other sleeve hangs over her shoulder and she clutches it to her heart.

There is no need for her to feel the way along the wall. There is no earthquake. Why does she move so slowly? Is that supposed to be a symbol of something? Why the fancy language, clutching things to hearts? Just the facts. What happens.

The mother rushes to the door and opens it. No doubt she has her dressing gown on properly. No one has said anything at all. It is the piano tuner at the door. He has come to tune the pianola. He has arrived early. 'It's an earthquake. Stay where you are,' the brother calls. He is laughing.

There is no earthquake. There are no earthquakes in this part of the world.

The piano tuner sniffs. 'What's the smell?' he asks. 'Not me, I didn't do it. I didn't make no smell,' says the brother. The daughter laughs. She thinks she will die of laughter. The mother turns her head slowly, more or less in the direction of her children.

There is no earthquake. No one is dizzy. Also inconsistent. The mother has already rushed to the door. There is no need for slow head turning, if any head turning at all.

The mother says, 'Don't speak that way in this house.' The brother says, 'I didn't do it, that's all I said.' The tears roll down his cheeks. The mother groans and leans against the wall. She shakes her head as if she has a drop of water in her ear. 'Where's your father?' she whispers. The brother says, 'When roses are red they're ready to pluck, when a girl's sixteen she's ready to drive a truck.' The mother says, 'You ought to be ashamed of yourself.'

No earthquake, no dizziness, no laughter, no elaboration, no metaphors. What happens.

The mother opens the door. It is the piano tuner. He has come to tune the pianola. He has arrived early. He says, 'What's the smell?' He walks past them into the kitchen. 'Everything's turned off in here.' He is checking the gas jets on the stove. 'What else have you got that's gas that could be leaking?' The mother replies, 'Everything in this house is gas. It's cheaper. We get the appliances at a discount. Everything's gas.'

The brother says, 'Appliances and people, both.' The piano tuner says, 'What about in the laundry?'

Enough with the reconstructed dialogue. The facts. What happens.

The piano tuner says he can smell gas. The mother runs into

40

the kitchen. She checks the gas jets. She throws open the windows and the back door. The piano tuner stays standing politely at the front door. The mother takes the daughter by the arm and leads her into the back garden. She leans her against the jacaranda tree and goes back to get the brother. The daughter holds on to the grey trunk and looks at the house. She sees the kitchen door painted blue, the window with her curtains, and the laundry door downstairs, also blue.

No trees, no doors, no curtains, no excursions into anyone's head. No fabrications. Only what happens. It does not matter, the tree or the colour blue. Forget the build-up and the climax. Just what happens.

The piano tuner stays at the front door. The mother rushes down the back steps to the laundry. The brother and daughter are following more slowly. The mother rushes back to the stairs and calls to the piano tuner to come and help. The daughter is at the top of the stairs and starts to come down. The mother orders her to stay where she is. The daughter walks on down and goes to the laundry door. There are rags and newspapers stuffed into the keyhole and the vents in the door and into the space between the door and the floor. The smell of gas is everywhere. The door is not locked. She pushes it open, coughing and retching at the gas. She holds her nose and goes in and turns off the laundry gas outlet which has been left on by mistake. Then they all go upstairs and wake the father up and they all have breakfast. The piano tuner tunes the pianola.

Not so. The pianola never got tuned.

The daughter stays at the top of the stairs, as she is told. The smell of gas is everywhere. It is the mother who rushes down the stairs and opens the laundry door. All the rags and newspapers fall to the floor. The father lies there on the laundry floor on a spare mattress that is stored in the laundry. His face is next to the outlet. He lies next to the dirty clothes. He looks as if he wants to be found in time. They drag him out into the air, near the jacaranda, and he revives.

No tree, no embellishments, no opinions, no lies.

It is a Tuesday morning. It is nine o'clock. The doorbell wakes them up. The smell of gas is everywhere. They have overslept, drugged by the gas. The mother opens the door. The Piano tuner has come, early. The mother rushes to the kitchen. She checks the gas jets. She opens the back door and rushes down to the laundry. The brother and daughter follow her. There are rags and newspapers stuffed into the keyhole and the vents in the door and into the space between the door and the floor. The door is not locked. The mother opens the door. The father lies there. He is dead, having gassed himself. Less than half a minute has passed since the doorbell rang. If the piano tuner had not come early, they would all be dead now.

Later they remember that the daughter was out late and was the last to go to bed. They ask why she did not notice the absence of the family joke and why she did not notice the smell of gas and why she did not avert the tragedy.

No, nobody actually asks anything like that. No need for denouement. This is an ordinary family, one of many such families in houses on streets. Nothing distinguishes it from the others, except, today, this event.

GRAHAM GREENE

The Case for the Defence

It was the strangest murder trial I ever attended. They named it the Peckham murder in the headlines, though Northwood Street, where the old woman was found battered to death, was not strictly speaking in Peckham. This was not one of those cases of circumstantial evidence in which you feel the jurymen's anxiety—because mistakes *have* been made—like domes of silence muting the court. No, this murderer was all but found with the body; no one present when the crown counsel outlined his case believed that the man in the dock stood any chance at all.

He was a heavy stout man with bulging bloodshot eyes. All his muscles seemed to be in his thighs. Yes, an ugly customer, one you wouldn't forget in a hurry—and that was an important point because the Crown proposed to call four witnesses who hadn't forgotten him, who had seen him hurrying away from the little red villa in Northwood Street. The clock had just struck two in the morning.

Mrs Salmon in 15 Northwood Street had been unable to sleep; she heard a door click shut and thought it was her own gate. So she went to the window and saw Adams (that was his name) on the steps of Mrs Parker's house. He had just come out and he was wearing gloves. He had a hammer in his hand and she saw him drop it into the laurel bushes by the front gate. But before he moved away, he had looked up—at her window. The fatal instinct that tells a man when he is watched exposed him in the light of a street-lamp to her gaze—his eyes suffused with horrifying and brutal fear, like an animal's when you raise a whip. I talked afterwards to Mrs Salmon, who naturally after the astonishing verdict went in fear herself. As I imagine did all the witnesses—Henry MacDougall, who had been driving home from Benfleet late and nearly ran Adams down at the corner of Northwood Street. Adams was walking in the middle of the road looking dazed. And old Mr Wheeler, who lived next door to Mrs Parker, at No. 12, and was wakened by a noise—like a chair falling—through the thin-as-paper villa wall, and got up and looked out of the window, just as Mrs Salmon had done, saw Adam's back and, as he turned, those bulging eyes. In Laurel Avenue he had been seen by yet another witness—his luck was badly out; he might as well have committed the crime in broad daylight.

'I understand,' counsel said, 'that the defence proposes to plead mistaken identity. Adams's wife will tell you that he was with her at two in the morning on February 14, but after you have heard the witnesses for the Crown and examined carefully the features of the prisoner, I do not think you will be prepared to admit the possibility of a mistake.'

It was all over, you would have said, but the hanging.

After the formal evidence had been given by the policeman who had found the body and the surgeon who examined it, Mrs Salmon was called. She was the ideal witness, with her slight Scotch accent and her expression of honesty, care and kindness.

The counsel for the Crown brought the story gently out. She spoke very firmly. There was no malice in her, and no sense of importance at standing there in the Central Criminal Court with a judge in scarlet hanging on her words and the reporters writing them down. Yes, she said, and then she had gone downstairs and rung up the police station.

'And do you see the man here in court?'

She looked straight at the big man in the dock, who stared hard at her with his pekingese eyes without emotion.

'Yes,' she said, 'there he is.'

'You are quite certain?'

She said simply, 'I couldn't be mistaken, sir.'

It was all as easy as that.

'Thank you, Mrs Salmon.'

Counsel for the defence rose to cross-examine. If you had reported as many murder trials as I have, you would have known beforehand what line he would take. And I was right, up to a point.

'Now, Mrs Salmon, you must remember that a man's life

may depend on your evidence.'

'I do remember it, sir.'

'Is your eyesight good?'

'I have never had to wear spectacles, sir.'

'You are a woman of fifty-five?'

'Fifty-six, sir.'

'And the man you saw was on the other side of the road?'

'Yes, sir.'

'And it was two o'clock in the morning. You must have remarkable eyes, Mrs Salmon?'

'No, sir. There was moonlight, and when the man looked up, he had the lamplight on his face.'

'And you have no doubt whatever that the man you saw is the prisoner?'

I couldn't make out what he was at. He couldn't have expected any other answer than the one he got.

'None whatever, sir. It isn't a face one forgets.'

Counsel took a look round the court for a moment. Then he said, 'Do you mind, Mrs Salmon, examining again the people in court? No, not the prisoner. Stand up, please, Mr Adams,' and there at the back of the court with thick stout body and muscular legs and a pair of bulging eyes, was the exact image of the man in the dock. He was even dressed the same—tight blue suit and striped tie.

'Now think very carefully, Mrs Salmon. Can you still swear that the man you saw drop the hammer in Mrs Parker's garden was the prisoner—and not this man who is his twin brother?'

Of course she couldn't. She looked from one to the other and didn't say a word.

There the big brute sat in the dock with his legs crossed and there he stood too at the back of the court and they both stared at Mrs Salmon. She shook her head.

What we saw then was the end of the case. There wasn't a witness prepared to swear that it was the prisoner he'd seen. And the brother? He had his alibi too; he was with his wife.

And so the man was acquitted for lack of evidence. But whether—if he did the murder and not his brother—he was punished or not, I don't know. That extraordinary day had an extraordinary end. I followed Mrs Salmon out of court and we got wedged in the crowd who were waiting, of course, for the twins. The police tried to draw the crowd away, but all they could do was keep the roadway clear for traffic. I learned later that they tried to get the twins to leave by a back way, but they wouldn't. One of them — no one knew which — said, 'I've been acquitted, haven't I?' and they walked bang out of the front entrance. Then it happened. I don't know how, though I was only six feet away. The crowd moved and somehow one of the twins got pushed on the road right in front of a bus.

He gave a squeal like a rabbit and that was all; he was dead, his skull smashed just as Mrs Parker's had been. Divine vengeance? I wish I knew. There was the other Adams getting on his feet from beside the body and looking straight over at Mrs Salmon. He was crying, but whether he was the murderer or the innocent man nobody will ever be able to tell. But if you were Mrs Salmon, could you sleep at night?

Bird Talk

The small kitchen was exactly as she had left it the night before. The tray laid, two upturned cups sitting squarely on their saucers. The full sugar basin with its clean spoon standing at the ready. The milk jug waiting to be filled and the tea caddy to hand at the side. Miriam picked up the kettle, and turning to the sink, filled it to precisely the right level and placed it on the gas stove. As she waited for the kettle to boil, Miriam mentally listed the endless chores for the day ahead.

Get father up. Wash him. Dress him. Feed him. Toilet him. Change his bed. Wash his clothes. Miriam's lips tightened as the list unfolded in her mind, deepening the lines etched around her mouth; lines formed by the effort of pursing her lips tightly to keep in the words she must not utter. The resentment against him began to grow again, and as it did, her large capable hands, with their scrupulously clean nails, began combing through her short grey hair, as if to calm the thoughts seething beneath.

It had been four long years now since that dreadful phone call, informing her of his illness.

'Your father has had a stroke' the ward sister had said, 'his condition is very serious, we don't expect he will recover consciousness.'

Miriam had hovered anxiously at his bedside for days. Listening in agony to his stertorous breathing. Watching closely for any sign of returning consciousness. Praying desperately for his recovery, and slowly, very slowly, he began to improve. He recovered consciousness, he moved his head and looked about him, he made strangled sorts of grunting noises, and Miriam rejoiced. The doctors and nursing staff were amazed by his recovery, and in no time at all it seemed, they were talking of his release from hospital.

Miriam, without hesitation, arranged for him to come and

47

stay with her. She would nurse him back to full health she'd thought. No matter if it meant giving up her job, she owed it to him. He'd been a good father to her, always providing a loving comfortable home. Making sure she had the best he was capable of providing. Caring for her through small troubles and large. Encouraging her in her chosen profession, and comforting her with his wise counsel when John, her husband, had died. Now she'd decided she could care for him, and so it was arranged. They brought him in an ambulance, on a stretcher, to her spare room, and Miriam began to nurse him.

As the days grew into weeks, and the weeks lengthened into months, it gradually became clear to her that in spite of her best efforts, he was not going to improve, and so arrangements were made to sell his house. He had lived alone since Miriam's mother had died some few years before. He had managed quite well really, and had seemed happy enough pottering about his small home, tending the garden and talking endlessly to his budgerigar, rewarded by the bird talking endlessly to him. It had fascinated Miriam to hear the two of them, the bird imitating her father's voice precisely. The bird and its cage were the only things salvaged from his home. Everything else was sold, but Miriam, in the forlorn hope that the talking bird might somehow help her father to speak again, installed it in his room.

He was completely paralysed down his right side, making feeding difficult and messy, and he was incontinent, doubly so some times. If he had regained his powers of speech perhaps things would have been different, but the grunting sounds he made were entirely unintelligible to Miriam and to everyone else who visited. Oddly the bird stopped talking too. Miriam talked to it often in the early days, but her words elicited no more response than her words to her father. Both man and bird remained speechless.

As the months dragged by with their endless monotonous routine of bathing, cleaning and feeding the old man, Miriam began to find it more and more difficult to identify him with the father she had known. This smelly, dribbling, grunting, demanding hulk, which she heaved daily from bed to chair and back again, bore no resemblance to the kind and thoughtful person that had been her father. That person had gone for ever, leaving this monstrosity behind. Ever more often Miriam found herself wishing he would die, and her forehead would contract, as if to squeeze out from her mind the awful wish.

Neighbours marvelled at her devotion.

'Don't know how you do it dear' they'd remark when they saw Miriam hanging out the endless washing, 'your mum would be real proud of you, one in a million you are. How is he then? Must pop in and see him soon.' But they never did, not now. At first she and her father had had lots of visitors. Friends and colleagues had called bearing gifts and good cheer. They would chat to Miriam, then go up to see her father.

'Hello there, how are you? You're looking better' they would say heartily, trying to ignore the sights of the sickroom and the lack of response. They would turn to the bird in the cage in an effort to relieve the embarrassment.

'Pretty boy' they would say, 'pretty boy, don't you talk any more?' and then turn away in even greater confusion at having made such a gaffe. Gradually they stopped visiting father and just dropped in on Miriam, but her cloistered world was so out of touch and different to their normality, that the gaps widened, visits became occasional phone calls, and even these had all but ceased.

Her aunts on their infrequent visits were full of praise for her. They would look in on her father, nodding and smiling to him, not speaking, knowing he couldn't answer. They would talk to the bird, recalling how well it had imitated the dozens of phrases her father had taught it.

'All very polite phrases too' remembered the aunts, and bemoaning the fact that it no longer entertained them with its talking, they'd make their way downstairs to rejoin Miriam.

'He's looking well' they'd say, 'you keep him really nice, you must feel proud of yourself, we know your mum would have been real pleased with you, God rest her soul.'

And they would drink the tea and eat the home-made scones, totally unaware of Miriam's situation.

The doctor too, on his weekly routine visits followed the same formula. A hearty 'How are you? you're looking well' followed by his standard joke to the bird. 'And how are you? So, you won't talk eh?'

'See you next week' to both bird and father, and off he would go downstairs to Miriam.

'Marvellous nurse you are m'dear, you've performed miracles, yes miracles, carry on like this and who knows, maybe you'll get both of them talking again.'

Miriam would shake her head deprecatingly. In the face of such universal praise, how could she tell them all how she really felt. How the sight and smell of him disgusted her. How she felt like a prisoner and him her jailer. It was impossible, she had to go on with the charade. Her only release would be his death.

Dispiritedly she removed the boiling kettle from the flame and made the tea. I will not lose my temper today, she resolved as she did each morning, then wearily she made her way upstairs. 'Let the bed be clean' she prayed to an unhearing Deity on the way. She spoke no word to her father. She had long since ceased to greet him or indeed converse with him at all, since he never appeared to respond in any intelligible way. Silently then she drew back the sheet. Thank goodness she thought, it's only wet, and she proceeded to remove the nightwear and sheets expertly from beneath the old man. He grunted incomprehensibly. Miriam looked at him. He appeared as a stranger to her.

'Die damn you die' Miriam said suddenly and explosively. The inner wish had been voiced once more. Miriam was instantly ashamed. Each day she strived to keep the words from utterance and almost each day she failed. Yet there was no one to hear, and she doubted her father could understand. Quickly she completed her task and covering him with clean sheets she gathered the soiled linen and made her way downstairs. The undrunk tea was too cold to be enjoyed now so Miriam made a fresh pot, poured her father's and once more climbed the stairs.

As soon as she entered the room she knew. She crossed quickly to the bed, and once more drew back the sheets. It was soiled. Miriam was exasperated. The day had hardly begun and already the bed had had to be changed twice. Roughly she removed the top sheet, then rolled the old man onto his side. In her anger she pushed rather than rolled, and the old man went right over, coming to rest with his face buried in one of his pillows. She knew he couldn't lift his head, and in a moment of madness she took up another pillow, and placing it over the back of his head, she pressed downward. How long she leaned over him pressing, she had no notion. Slowly she straightened and looked down at the still and silent form. Tentatively she turned him onto his back. He made no movement. He was dead. Miriam looked down at him, suddenly seeing him in death as her father again. Quietly she began to weep.

Presently she pulled herself together. She must phone the doctor. She wondered if he would suspect. How awful if he should know, if anyone should know, she could never bear the shame of it, she would have to convince the doctor that it was a natural death. She squared her shoulders and went downstairs to phone.

The doctor came quickly, and after a brief examination turned to Miriam.

'He's gone I'm afraid' he said kindly to her, placing his arm across her shoulders, as she began to cry. 'Come my dear, you've nothing to reproach yourself with, you've been devoted to him. Just sit down here whilst I write out the death certificate.'

Miriam sat down as the doctor took out his pen and the pad of death certificates. It was very quiet, the only sound in the room was the scratch of the pen on the paper, when suddenly the bird fluttered on its perch in the cage.

'Die damn you die,' it said loudly and clearly in unmistakable imitation of Miriam.

'Die damn you die' over and over again.

RICHARD BRAUTIGAN
The Scarlatti Tilt

'It's very hard to live in a studio apartment in San Jose with a man who's learning to play the violin.' That's what she told the police when she handed them the empty revolver.

ANON
The Spirit of the Law

An American who had established a flourishing business in England ran into a spot of trouble and went to an English friend for advice. 'Say, Rodney,' he began, 'I'm in a bit of a jam. I've got a customer who threatens to take me to court, and I'm afraid he's got a pretty good case.' He went into the details of the case, and concluded: 'Do you think it would be a good idea for me to slip the judge a bottle or two of whisky?'

Rodney was horrified. 'Good Lord, old man, you mustn't do that! I can't think of anything more likely to turn the judge against you. Why, that'd be the best way to lose, old boy.'

A month or so later Rodney was somewhat surprised to hear that his American friend had won the case, so he phoned him up and asked how it had come about.

'Gee,' replied the American, 'it was a cinch. I sent the judge a crate of whisky and put the other guy's name on it.'

CYRIL HARE

The Old Flame

To commit a murder on a Bank Holiday at a popular seaside resort in broad daylight argues a good deal of courage, of a sort; but courage was the one good quality in which Jack Saunders was not deficient.

In fact, when he began to make his plans for the elimination of Maggie, he soon realised that, as so often happens, the boldest course was the safest.

In some ways he genuinely regretted the necessity of what he was about to do, but once he had recognised that Maggie was an insurmountable obstacle to his career, he firmly put any useless repining to one side.

A phrase from a bit of poetry learned by heart at school—that must have been in his last term before he was expelled—came faintly back to his memory. Something about rising on stepping stones of our dead selves to higher things. It seemed oddly appropriate—with this important difference, that it was on the stepping stone of Maggie's dead self that he proposed to rise.

As to the higher things — they, of course, were represented by Mary Rossiter—Mary and her money and her absurdly gullible family, who had taken him at his face value and accepted him as Mary's fiancé without making the smallest inquiry into his past. Saunders could not but grin when he thought of the Rossiters.

They would be sailing back to Australia once they had seen their daughter wedded to the gentlemanly Englishman who had been so kind and useful to them during their visit to the old country. They were in Paris now, buying Mary's trousseau, and he was to join them there for a little holiday—at their expense, of course.

Once the wedding was over they would not trouble him, but Maggie would—Maggie with her prison record as an

53

expert sneak thief and pickpocket and, what was worse, her knowledge of his prison record.

It had been all that he could do to keep her in the background while he was cultivating the acquaintance of the Rossiters. Already she had tried a little gentle blackmail. Decidedly, there was not room in his life for Maggie and Mary.

And so to Bank Holiday, the day on which Saunders was to sail to meet the Rossiters in Paris, the day which he had decided on as Maggie's last.

To all appearances, nothing could have been more innocent than the little jaunt to the seaside that he proposed, and with which Maggie, who had been pestering him for his company for some time, fell in so readily.

Nothing more innocent than the elderly family saloon in which they pottered in an endless string of other elderly family saloons along the road to the coast that morning. (Somewhere a family was wondering what had become of their saloon, which they had incautiously left unattended in the West End overnight. It had fresh number plates now and a skilfully altered licence.)

Nothing more natural than that the drive should have ended on the downs overlooking the harbour where the Channel boat was making ready to sail. And if the couple in the car chose to recline on the back seat very close in each other's arms, well, could anything be more natural than that?

There was a sharp breeze blowing in from the sea across the top of the hill, and the car was only one of dozens parked near by, occupied by other couples similarly employed.

A flight of jet aircraft screamed overhead. Under cover of the sound Saunders slipped out of the car.

By the time that the heads and eyes of the throng of holiday-makers had turned from following them, he was yards away from it, an inconspicuous unit in the mass, making his way down a cliff path towards the sea.

It had been extraordinarily easy, he told himself—so easy that he almost felt apologetic towards the girl who had allowed herself to be snuffed out with so little trouble.

She had guessed, as he had expected that she would, that this Bank Holiday outing was in the nature of a farewell; but as he had not expected, she had not made a scene when she realised it.

It was the only respect in which things had not gone exactly according to plan.

He had braced himself for a quarrel, but there had been none. The foul-mouthed little thief had been sweet forgiveness itself.

She had only asked for a last kiss. And what a kiss! Saunders's lips still tingled with it as he strode nonchalantly along.

Which, of course, had made things childishly simple. A commando training in unarmed combat qualified a man to do harder things than squeezing the life out of a girl already limp and helpless in one's arms.

It was simply a matter of remembering one's instructions about pressure points...

All the same, it was a pity. Maggie must have loved him after all. Mary would never learn to kiss like that. Perhaps he had been wrong and could have kept them both. For a moment Saunders wondered whether it had been right to murder Maggie.

Still keeping up his unhurried stroll, Saunders approached the harbour. He had worked to a careful timetable, and like everything else on this successful day, it fitted perfectly.

The boat-train was just coming in. A flood of chattering tourists surged towards the Customs sheds. Saunders allowed himself to be caught up in the crowd and waited patiently as it marshalled itself into the inevitable queue.

Slowly now, step by step, they moved forward, jostling, laughing, bumping one another with their suitcases and haversacks. Somewhere ahead a tired voice was chanting: 'British passports this way! Have your passports ready, please!'

It was not until he had nearly reached the barrier that Saunders felt in his breast pocket—felt once, twice and yet again in desperate unbelief. Then he fell out of the queue and began to go through all the pockets in his suit, in vain.

He tore open the little handbag that he carried and found nothing there but his things for a night or two away from home.

'Have your passports ready, please!' the voice repeated just over his head. 'British passports this way!'

A long time after, it seemed to Saunders, another voice close by said to him,

'Lost your passport, sir? That's a bit of bad luck. Perhaps you had your pocket picked? It happens here sometimes, you know.'

Saunders nodded dumbly. He could still feel Maggie's arms as they went tenderly round him in that last, close embrace.

'Afraid you can't go on board without a passport,' the voice went on. 'Spoiled your holiday, I'm afraid. But I shouldn't worry too much, sir, just give the particulars in at the office. The police will find it all right.'

And sure enough, they did.

The Man with the Scar

It was on account of the scar that I first noticed him, for it ran, broad and red, in a great crescent from his temple to his chin. It must have been due to a formidable wound and I wondered whether this had been caused by a sabre or by a fragment of shell. It was unexpected on that round, fat, and good-humoured face. He had small and undistinguished features, and his expression was artless. His face went oddly with his corpulent body. He was a powerful man of more than common height. I never saw him in anything but a very shabby grey suit, a khaki shirt, and a battered sombrero. He was far from clean. He used to come into the Palace Hotel at Guatemala City every day at cocktail time and strolling leisurely round the bar offer lottery tickets for sale. If this was the way he made his living it must have been a poor one for I never saw anyone buy, but now and then I saw him offered a drink. He never refused it. He threaded his way among the tables with a sort of rolling walk as though he were accustomed to traverse long distances on foot, paused at each table, with a little smile mentioned the numbers he had for sale, and then, when no notice was taken of him, with the same smile passed on. I think he was for the most part a trifle the worse for liquor.

I was standing at the bar one evening, my foot on the rail, with an acquaintance—they make a very good dry Martini at the Palace Hotel in Guatemala City—when the man with the scar came up. I shook my head as for the twentieth time since my arrival he held out for my inspection his lottery tickets. But my companion nodded affably.

'*Qué tal, general*? How is life?'

'Not so bad. Business is none too good, but it might be worse.'

'What will you have, general?'

'A brandy.'

He tossed it down and put the glass back on the bar. He nodded to my acquaintance.

'*Gracias. Hasta luego.*'

Then he turned away and offered his tickets to the men who were standing next to us.

'Who is your friend?' I asked. 'That's a terrific scar on his face.'

'It doesn't add to his beauty, does it? He's an exile from Nicaragua. He's a ruffian of course and a bandit, but not a bad fellow. I give him a few *pesos* now and then. He was a revolutionary general, and if his ammunition hadn't given out he'd have upset the government and be Minister of War now instead of seelling lottery tickets in Guatemala. They captured him, along with his staff, such as it was, and tried him by court-martial. Such things are rather summary in these countries, you know, and he was sentenced to be shot at dawn. I guess he knew what was coming to him when he was caught. He spent the night in gaol and he and the others, there were five of them altogether, passed the time playing poker. They used matches for chips. He told me he'd never had such a run of bad luck in his life; they were playing with a short pack, Jacks to open, but he never held a card; he never improved more than half a dozen times in the whole sitting and no sooner did he buy a new stack than he lost it. When day broke and the soldiers came into the cell to fetch them for execution he had lost more matches than a reasonable man could use in a lifetime.

'They were led into the patio of the gaol and placed against a wall, the five of them side by side, with the firing party facing them. There was a pause and our friend asked the officer in charge of them what the devil they were keeping him waiting for. The officer said that the general commanding the government troops wished to attend the execution and they awaited his arrival.

'"Then I have time to smoke another cigarette," said our friend. "He was always unpunctual."'

'But he had barely lit it when the general—it was San Ignacio, by the way: I don't know whether you ever met him—followed by his ADC came into the patio. The usual formalities

58

were performed and San Ignacio asked the condemned men whether there was anything they wished before the execution took place. Four of the five shook their heads, but our friend spoke.

'"Yes, I should like to say good-bye to my wife."'

'"*Bueno*," said the general, "I have no objection to that. Where is she?"'

'"She is waiting at the prison door."'

'"Then it will not cause a delay of more than five minutes."'

'"Hardly that, *Señor General*," said our friend.'

'"Have him placed on one side."'

'Two soldiers advanced and between them the condemned rebel walked to the spot indicated. The officer in command of the firing squad on a nod from the general gave an order, there was a ragged report, and the four men fell. They fell strangely, not together, but one after the other, with movements that were almost grotesque, as though they were puppets in a toy theatre. The officer went up to them and into one who was still alive emptied two barrels of his revolver. Our friend finished his cigarette and threw away the stub.

'There was a little stir at the gateway. A woman came into the patio, with quick steps, and then, her hand on her heart, stopped suddenly. She gave a cry and with outstretched arms ran forward.

'"*Caramba*," said the General.

'She was in black, with a veil over her hair, and her face was dead white. She was hardly more than a girl, a slim creature, with little regular features and enormous eyes. But they were distraught with anguish. Her loveliness was such that as she ran, her mouth slightly open and the agony of her face beautiful, a gasp of surprise was wrung from those indifferent soldiers who looked at her.

'The rebel advanced a step or two to meet her. She flung herself into his arms and with a hoarse cry of passion: *alma de mi corazón*, soul of my heart, he pressed his lips to hers. And at the same moment he drew a knife from his ragged shirt—I haven't a notion how he managed to retain possession of it—and stabbed her in the neck. The blood spurted from the cut vein and dyed his shirt. Then he flung his arms round her and once more pressed his lips to hers.

'It happened so quickly that many did not know what had occurred, but from the others burst a cry of horror; they sprang forward and seized him. They loosened his grasp and the girl would have fallen if the ADC had not caught her. She was unconscious. They laid her on the ground and with dismay on their faces stood round watching her. The rebel knew where he was striking and it was impossible to staunch the blood. In a moment the ADC who had been kneeling by her side rose.

'"She's dead," he whispered.

'The rebel crossed himself.

'"Why did you do it?" asked the general.

'"I loved her."

'A sort of sigh passed through those men crowded together and they looked with strange faces at the murderer. The general stared at him for a while in silence.

'"It was a noble gesture," he said at last. "I cannot execute this man. Take my car and have him led to the frontier. *Señor*, I offer you the homage which is due from one brave man to another."

'A murmur of approbation broke from those who listened. The ADC tapped the rebel on the shoulder, and between the two soldiers without a word he marched to the waiting car.'

My friend stopped and for a little I was silent. I must explain that he was a Guatemalecan and spoke to me in Spanish. I have translated what he told me as well as I could, but I have made no attempt to tone down his rather high-flown language. To tell the truth I think it suits the story.

'But how then did he get the scar?' I asked at length.

'Oh, that was due to a bottle that burst when I was opening it. A bottle of ginger ale.'

'I never liked it,' said I.

HENRY SLEASAR

Examination Day

The Jordans never spoke of the exam, not until their son, Dickie, was 12 years old. It was on his birthday that Mrs Jordan first mentioned the subject in his presence, and the anxious manner of her speech caused her husband to answer sharply.

'Forget about it,' he said. 'He'll do all right.'

They were at the breakfast table, and the boy looked up from his plate curiously. He was an alert-eyed youngster, with flat blond hair and a quick, nervous manner. He didn't understand what the sudden tension was about, but he did know that today was his birthday, and he wanted harmony above all. Somewhere in the little apartment there were wrapped, be-ribboned packages waiting to be opened, and in the tiny wall- kitchen, something warm and sweet was being prepared in the automatic stove. He wanted the day to be happy, and the moistness of his mother's eyes, the scowl on his father's face, spoiled the mood of fluttering expectation with which he had greeted the morning.

'What exam?' he asked.

His mother looked at the tablecloth. 'It's just a sort of Government intelligence test they give children at the age of 12. You'll be taking it next week. It's nothing to worry about.'

'You mean a test like in school?'

'Something like that,' his father said, getting up from the table. 'Go and read your comics, Dickie.' The boy rose and wandered towards that part of the living room which had been 'his' corner since infancy. He fingered the topmost comic of the stack, but seemed uninterested in the colourful squares of fast-paced action. He wandered towards the window, and peered gloomily at the veil of mist that shrouded the glass.

'Why did it have to rain today?' he said. 'Why couldn't it rain tomorrow?'

His father, now slumped into an armchair with the Government newspaper, rattled the sheets in vexation. 'Because it just did, that's all. Rain makes the grass grow.'

'Why, Dad?'

'Because it does, that's all.'

Dickie puckered his brow. 'What makes it green, though? The grass?'

'Nobody knows,' his father snapped, then immediately regretted his abruptness.

Later in the day, it was birthday time again. His mother beamed as she handed over the gaily-coloured packages, and even his father managed a grin and a rumple-of-the-hair. He kissed his mother and shook hands gravely with his father. Then the birthday cake was brought forth, and the ceremonies concluded.

An hour later, seated by the window he watched the sun force its way between the clouds.

'Dad' he said, 'how far away is the sun?'

'Five thousand miles,' his father said.

Dickie sat at the breakfast table and again saw moisture in his mother's eyes. He didn't connect her tears with the exam until his father suddenly brought the subject to light again.

'Well, Dickie,' he said, with a manly frown. 'You've got an appointment today.'

'I know Dad. I hope—'

'Now, it's nothing to worry about. Thousands of children take this test every day. The Government wants to know how smart you are, Dickie. That's all there is to it.'

'I get good marks in school,' he said hesitantly.

'This is different. This is a—special kind of test. They give you this stuff to drink, you see, and then you go into a room where there's a sort of machine—'

'What stuff to drink?' Dickie said.

'It's nothing. It tastes like peppermint. It's just to make sure you answer the questions truthfully. Not that the Government thinks you won't tell the truth, but this stuff makes *sure*.'

Dickie's face showed puzzlement, and a touch of fright. He looked at his mother, and she composed her face into a misty smile.

'Everything will be all right,' she said.

'Of course it will,' his father agreed. 'You're a good boy, Dickie; you'll make out fine. Then we'll come home and celebrate. All right?'

'Yes, sir,' Dickie said.

They entered the Government Educational Building fifteen minutes before the appointed hour. They crossed the marble floors of the great pillared lobby, passed beneath an archway and entered an automatic lift that brought them to the fourth floor.

There was a young man wearing an insignia-less tunic, seated at a polished desk in front of Room 404. He held a clipboard in his hand, and he checked the list down to the Js and permitted the Jordans to enter.

The room was as cold and official as a courtroom, with long benches flanking metal tables. There were several fathers and sons already there, and a thin-lipped woman with cropped black hair was passing out sheets of paper.

Mr Jordan filled out the form, and returned it to the clerk. Then he told Dickie: 'It won't be long now. When they call your name, you just go through the doorway at that end of the room.' He indicated the portal with his finger.

A concealed loudspeaker crackled and called off the first name. Dickie saw a boy leave his father's side reluctantly and walk slowly towards the door.

At five minutes to eleven, they called the name of Jordan.

'Good luck, son,' his father said, without looking at him. 'I'll call for you when the test is over.'

Dickie walked to the door and turned the knob. The room inside was dim, and he could barely make out the features of the grey-tunicked attendant who greeted him.

'Sit down,' the man said softly. He indicated a high stool beside his desk. 'Your name's Richard Jordan?'

'Yes, sir.'

'Your classification number is 600—115. Drink this, Richard.'

He lifted a plastic cup from the desk and handed it to the boy. The liquid inside had the consistency of buttermilk, tasted only vaguely of the promised peppermint. Dickie downed it, and handed the man the empty cup.

He sat in silence, feeling drowsy, while the man wrote

busily on a sheet of paper. Then the attendant looked at his watch, and rose to stand only inches from Dickie's face. He unclipped a penlike object from the pocket of his tunic, and flashed a tiny light into the boy's eyes.

'All right,' he said. 'Come with me, Richard.'

He led Dickie to the end of the room, where a single wooden armchair faced a multi-dialled computing machine. There was a microphone on the left arm of the chair, and when the boy sat down, he found its pinpoint head conveniently at his mouth.

'Now just relax, Richard. You'll be asked some questions, and you think them over carefully. Then give your answers into the microphone. The machine will take care of the rest.'

'Yes, sir.'

'I'll leave you alone now. Whenever you want to start, just say "ready" into the microphone.'

'Yes, sir.'

The man squeezed his shoulder, and left.

Dickie said, 'Ready.'

Lights appeared on the machine, and a mechanism whirred. A voice said:

'Complete this sequence. One, four, seven, ten...'

Mr and Mrs Jordan were in the living room, not speaking, not even speculating.

It was almost four o'clock when the telephone rang. The woman tried to reach it first, but her husband was quicker.

'Mr Jordan?'

The voice was clipped; a brisk, official voice.

'Yes, speaking.'

This is the Government Educational Service. Your son, Richard M. Jordan, Classification 600—115, has completed the Government examination. We regret to inform you that his intelligence quotient is above the Government regulation, according to Rule 84, Section 5, of the New Code.'

Across the room, the woman cried out, knowing nothing except the emotion she read on her husband's face.

'You may specify by telephone,' the voice droned on, 'whether you wish his body interred by the Government, or would you prefer a private burial place? The fee for Government burial is ten dollars.'

Nice and Hygienic

'By God, I could kill her!' Mr Henry Fairwell spoke his thought aloud, sitting up abruptly in his armchair.

'Sir?' purred the butler, at his elbow.

'Nothing, Hudson,' said Mr Fairwell, slumping back, a dried-bundle-of-sticks man.

'As you wish, sir.' Fattish, oil-jointed Hudson sank heavy steps into the deep pile of the carpet, pawed open the Adam door, and went backstairs.

'He could kill her!' Cook told Hudson. 'I've seen his eyes.'

'So?' said Hudson.

Cook shook indignant rolls of plumpness at the butler. Her eyes caught fire:

'She treats him worse than a dog! All that money and he never has a penny. All she gives him is her tongue.'

'She makes it,' said Hudson.

'With his companies,' said Cook.

'She's trebled his fortune—in oil, in tin, in rubber. She has a most astute business brain.'

'His fortune! His money!' Cook opened wide, tuppenny-weekly eyes, imaginatively dilated by such fare. 'He'll kill her yet, mark my words. Or he'd like to.'

'The last is perhaps nearer to the mark in my estimation,' said Hudson, sleekly moving away. He permitted himself a Cheshire grin as, businesslike, he made a telephone call. His large green jungle eyes narrowed their lids and inwardly he saw the rat-tail twitch of dollar signs.

Mr Fairwell, spare, fiftyish, pickled dry with hate, sat up suddenly in his armchair. In front of the Sheraton cabinet a royal-blue cloud floated. It flared to purple and dissolved in brown smoke.

'I say!' said Mr Fairwell.

The smoke had resolved itself into a man, lean-faced and olive-skinned. He was dressed in black, rather like battle dress.

'I don't believe it!' said Mr Fairwell. 'I'm dreaming.'

'You have never been so wide awake, my dear sir,' said the man. 'Allow me to present myself.'

He walked over to Mr Fairwell, holding out a white card. In his other hand he held a small camera-like instrument. From it came a soft whirring sound and in the lozenge-shaped glass at the front, spectrum ranges of colours showed briefly, pursuing each other.

Mr Fairwell took the card, read:

MURDER INCORPORATED
Founded AD 2180
100 Years of Service Behind Us
Representative: G. Turk

'This,' said Mr Fairwell, firmly, 'is some sort of practical joke. But I am not in the mood.' He reached out a hand to the scarlet bell-rope. 'I shall call Hudson to have you thrown out —and I shall dismiss Hudson for letting you in to see me.'

'If your wife permits,' said the visitor. 'There would be no point in calling Hudson as may be presently clear to you. I am Turk of Murder Incorporated. I have come back from the Future to do you a little favour—for a consideration, of course.' He coughed in mock embarrassment. 'To come to the point, I gather you would like your wife—er—eliminated?'

Mr Fairwell didn't answer but his eyes opened wide momentarily. The man waited, raised black bat's-wing eyebrows. 'How can I convince you of my bona fides? I realise, of course, that this outfit is a bit overdone—' here he touched his sinister suit— 'for a man as intelligent as yourself. But with the less intelligent, I assure you, it is most impressive.' He coughed. 'Black for death, you know. To business, sir! Murder Incorporated is at your service. I have come back from AD 2280 to eliminate your wife for you for a consideration. Shall we say, ten thousand dollars? The job will be carried out with spare and brilliant efficiency; no suspicion will attach to you—or, if there is, no harm will come to you. We guarantee that.'

Mr Fairwell's face purpled. You are some sort of maniac, sir. I am devoted to my wife. Now—'

He reached again for the bell-rope. At the same instant the visitor moved his hands about the camera-shaped box he was carrying.

'I shall have to establish my bona fides,' he murmured.

A purple ray hissed out of the box and spread into a cloud; then the cloud turned royal blue. The cloud sped out of the room and took with it Mr Fairwell and the holder of the box.

Time sped for Mr Fairwell. It whirled like a film run fantastically, inconceivably fast. Suns rose in a tenth of a second and splutteringly died in as brief an instant.

The room lay empty in the afternoon sun. A bee found a way in over the sill and flew into the room. Then it sought to escape. It butted against the window-pane for ten minutes.

'Do you see that bee?' asked Turk. He and Mr Fairwell had just returned.

Mr Fairwell nodded.

'Nasty little things, bees, I trust that my little demonstration has convinced you of my bona fides?'

Mr Fairwell nodded enthusiastically. 'Most emphatically. My head is still reeling though. It's incredible.'

'Nasty bee,' said Turk, 'Perhaps I could demonstrate on it how a certain person could be hygienically eliminated.'

'You did suggest another method,' said Fairwell, from behind his desk. 'You said that Emily could be transported into the Future — just as I was a few minutes ago.'

'Elimination is less troublesome,' said Turk. 'Allow me to demonstrate.'

He pointed the box at the bee. A red angry ray struck out. Around the bee there was a sudden green-blue flare like a shorting light-switch. A small green cloud melted and was gone.

'Nothing,' said Turk. 'Disintegrated. Even the atoms broken down. Absolute. Hygienic. No smell. No evidence. It was and now it isn't. Transportation is troublesome and it isn't absolute. Transport your wife and I haven't really done my job— she's still alive. It makes our name, Murder Incorporated, seem silly—I'm sorry now I mentioned the alternative.'

'I think I would prefer transportation,' said Mr Fairwell. 'Killing is too good for Emily. I want to think of her dumped in the Future and bewailing the loss of her financial empire.' Mr Fairwell tapped on the desk with long finger-nails and then athletically walked his fingers over the glassy surface. 'You are clear on the point that I cannot pay you ten thousand dollars until Emily is—er—out of the way.'

'Perfectly,' said Turk.

'To show I'm not a difficult man. I'll make it fifteen thousand dollars for you to transport her.'

'All right,' said Turk, slowly, 'transportation it is, though mind you, the other method is more efficient.'

'Transport Emily to the most barren and desolate part of the Future you can devise,' said Fairwell. 'You mentioned a safeguard, should suspicion fall on me?'

'I intended to mention that,' said Turk. 'In the unlikely event of your being, say, in prison or in the death cell—' Mr Fairwell shuddered— 'I shall personally see to your safety. I shall snatch you from the hangman's noose. You shall cheat Eternity by jaunting into the Future. We guarantee all our clients. Fear nothing. We have agents to keep us informed.'

Mr Fairwell mopped his head. 'It's a relief to know this.'

'One little point,' said Turk. 'I must regretfully inform you that you will shortly lose Hudson. There's other work—'

'Is he—?' began Mr Fairwell.

'He's one of us,' said Turk. 'On commission for the jobs he finds.'

Mr and Mrs Fairwell were eating breakfast in the holiday hotel in Arizona. Mrs Fairwell picked vulturishly at a grapefruit. Mr Fairwell nibbled his, canary-wise. Through the wide window lay the desert, brown and naked. White rapids of mirages ran in the mid-morning sun.

'I will give this photographer ten minutes only,' said Emily Fairwell.

'It may be enough,' said Mr Fairwell.

'Henry, why are you smiling?' cried short Mrs Fairwell, biting steely jaws and patting dark shining hair.

'Did I smile?' asked Mr Fairwell, mildly.

Outside, the brown-red rocks wobbled in the heat haze like an ill-tuned television picture.

'You did!' said Emily Fairwell. 'I'm not imaginative but it was a nasty smile—like the time when I caught you whipping dear little Flossie.'

'That was a nasty little dog,' said Mr Fairwell. He was feeling daring this morning. Normally he would never have spoken this way.

'Henry!' cried Mrs Fairwell for the second time that morning. 'Ten minutes is all I can allow that Mr Turk. He was so persistent. A "Genius of Finance" he called me. He thinks I'll be in *Life*.'

'Ha, ha,' laughed Mr Fairwell, inside.

'He can take me during my ride in the desert this morning,' said Mrs Fairwell.

'Yes,' said Mr Fairwell.

Mr Fairwell, sixtyish, not so spare as he had once been, now blandly preserved in good living, dozed in his armchair and then sat up suddenly. In front of the Sheraton cabinet a royal-blue cloud floated. It flared to purple and dissolved in brown smoke.

The smoke flew together.

'It's no use attempting to blackmail me, Turk,' said Mr Fairwell. 'I rather thought you might try though really, after ten years—' Mr Fairwell spread plump complacent hands.

'Not blackmail,' said Turk. He waved the box in which the colours of the spectrum gyrated slowly. 'It's another commission. Elimination. Clean and hygienic.'

'That's different,' said Mr Fairwell. 'I'm glad to see you dear fellow, in that case.'

'I hardly think you will when you learn whom I am acting for—I'm acting for your wife.'

Mr Fairwell paled. 'For Emily?'

Turk nodded. Mr Fairwell pulled himself up in his armchair. 'I'll double anything she has offered you,' he said, tugging the words out of himself.

Turk shook his head.

'Fifty thousand dollars!' said Mr Fairwell. 'No? One hundred thousand then! Not enough? I can outbid her. Anything you name! Name it!'

Turk said: 'You couldn't name it, sir. It'd be worth more than my life to do what you say. This is an order from up top.'

'Emily—' gasped Mr Fairwell. 'She's not—?'

'Head of MI,' said Turk. 'A financial genius!' His hands moved over the box.

ISAAC ASIMOV

The Fun They Had

Margie even wrote about it that night in her diary. On the page headed 17 May, 2155, she wrote, 'Today Tommy found a real book!

It was a very old book. Margie's grandfather once said that when he was a little boy *his* grandfather told him that there was a time when all stories were printed on paper.

They turned the pages, which were yellow and crinkly, and it was awfully funny to read words that stood still instead of moving the way they were supposed to—on a screen, you know. And then, when they turned back to the page before, it had the same words on it that it had had when they read it the first time.

'Gee,' said Tommy, 'what a waste. When you're through with the book, you just throw it away, I guess. Our television screen must have had a million books on it and it's good for plenty more. I wouldn't throw *it* away.'

'Same with mine,' said Margie. She was eleven and hadn't seen as many telebooks as Tommy had. He was thirteen.

She said, 'Where did you find it?'

'In my house.' He pointed without looking, because he was busy reading. 'In the attic.'

'What's it about?'

'School.'

Margie was scornful. 'School? What's there to write about school? I hate school.' Margie always hated school, but now she hated it more than ever. The mechanical teacher had been giving her test after test in geography and she had been doing worse and worse until her mother had shaken her head sorrowfully and sent for the County Inspector.

He was a round little man with a red face and a whole box of tools with dials and wires. He smiled at her and gave her an apple, then took the teacher apart. Margie had hoped he

71

wouldn't know how to put it together again, but he knew how all right and after an hour or so, there it was again, large and black and ugly with a big screen on which all the lessons were shown and the questions were asked. That wasn't so bad. The part she hated most was the slot where she had to put homework and test papers. She always had to write them out in a punch code they made her learn when she was six years old, and the mechanical teacher calculated the mark in no time.

The Inspector had smiled after he was finished and patted her head. He said to her mother, 'It's not the little girl's fault, Mrs Jones. I think the geography sector was geared a little too quick. Those things happen sometimes. I've slowed it up to an average ten-year level. Actually, the overall pattern of her progress is quite satisfactory.' And he patted Margie's head again.

Margie was disappointed. She had been hoping they would take the teacher away altogether. They had once taken Tommy's teacher away for nearly a month because the history sector had blanked out completely.

So she said to Tommy, 'Why would anyone write about school?'

Tommy looked at her with very superior eyes. 'Because it's not our kind of school, stupid. This is the old kind of school that they had hundreds and hundreds of years ago.' He added loftily, pronouncing the word carefully, '*Centuries* ago.'

Margie was hurt. 'Well, I don't know what kind of school they had all that time ago.' She read the book over his shoulder for a while, then said, 'Anyway, they had a teacher.'

'Sure they had a teacher, but it wasn't a *regular* teacher. It was a man.'

'A man? How could a man be a teacher?'

'Well, he just told the boys and girls things and gave them homework and asked them questions.'

'A man isn't smart enough.'

'Sure he is. My father knows as much as my teacher.'

'He can't. A man can't know as much as a teacher.'

'He knows almost as much I betcha.'

Margie wasn't prepared to dispute that. She said, 'I

wouldn't want a strange man in my house to teach me.'

Tommy screamed with laughter. 'You don't know much, Margie. The teachers didn't live in the house. They had a special building and all the kids went there.'

'And all the kids learned the same thing?'

'Sure, if they were the same age.'

'But my mother says a teacher had to be adjusted to fit the mind of each boy and girl it teaches and that each kid has to be taught differently.'

'Just the same they didn't do it that way then. If you don't like it, you don't have to read the book.'

'I didn't say I didn't like it,' Margie said quickly. She wanted to read about those funny schools.

They weren't even half finished when Margie's mother called, 'Margie! School!'

Margie looked up. 'Not yet, mamma.'

'Now,' said Mrs Jones. 'And it's probably time for Tommy, too.

Margie said to Tommy. 'Can I read the book some more with you after school?'

'Maybe,' he said nonchalantly. He walked away whistling, the dusty old book tucked beneath his arm.

Margie went into the schoolroom. It was right next to her bedroom, and the mechanical teacher was on and waiting for her. It was always on at the same time every day except Saturday and Sunday, because her mother said little girls learned better if they learned at regular hours.

The screen was lit up, and it said: 'Today's arithmetic lesson is on the addition of proper fractions. Please insert yesterday's homework in the proper slot.

Margie did so with a sigh. She was thinking about the old schools they had when her grandfather's grandfather was a little boy. All the kids from the whole neighbourhood came, laughing and shouting in the school-yard, sitting together in the school-room, going home together at the end of the day. They learned the same things so they could help one another on the homework and talk about it.

And the teachers were people...

The mechanical teacher was flashing on the screen: 'When we add the fractions ½ and ¼ —'

Margie was thinking about how the kids must have loved it in the old days. She was thinking about they fun they had.

GARY KILWORTH
Murderers Walk

Place

There is a city-state, lying between two large countries, where killers take refuge from the law, but not from justice. Justice finds its own way.

A long street, not much wider than an alley, cuts through the middle of the city. The street is called Murderers Walk and over its cobbles, slick even on dry days, tread the malefactors who have run to its shadows to escape the rope.

The houses are old and overhang the walk, keeping it permanently in the shade. Along its cobbles it is not unusual to see a man or woman being dragged, or driven, or forcibly carried. Sometimes they are screaming; sometimes they are stiff with fear.

Rope

There are many reminders of rope in Murderers Walk. The limbs of those lounging in apathy against crumbling window-sills are knotted and sinuous; the washing over the street is crowded onto short lines and consequently hangs narrow and long; the shadows that ripple in the poorly-fashioned windows tend to be thin and twisted due to the warping of the glass. A walk along the street on any day will bring you into contact with men and women who know death first-hand: they have dealt with it directly; they stand on the brink of death themselves. You see them waiting in shop doorways, wearing hollows in the wood with restless shoulders. No one knows what or who they are waiting for — not even those who wait. There is no expectancy in the air.

The Game

They play a game in the inns along Murderers Walk, which newcomers shun when they first arrive. Newcomers are detached and need nothing but themselves. They are either elated or relieved at having escaped the law in their own countries, and for a time this is sufficient to sustain them. The game is played in groups of nine, called 'scaffolds'.

The Rules

Each player draws cards from the pack containing two jokers, until none remain. The players look at their hands and the one holding the ace of spades must commit suicide, by hanging, twenty-four hours later, on the stroke of 8 am. It is a simple game, with simple rules, but the winning players recharge those feelings of elation and relief that they felt on first arriving in Murderers Walk. They have beaten death yet again.

The Victim

The players keep all their cards secret until the time arrives to take account. They gather at the inn where the game took place. One of the players will be missing and he or she will hold the ace of spades. The other players then go to the victim's rooms to witness the self-inflicted execution. Victims who are not ready at the appointed time are hunted down by the scaffold and the deed is done for them.

Alternative

There is an alternative to suicide. The victims can leave the city-state and the sanctuary of Murderers Walk to take their chances with the law on the outside. Not many do. It is not fear of death that is responsible but terror of dying in the hands of strangers: a ritual death conceived by a morality since rejected. It is a repulsion stronger than the fear of suicide.

Reprieve

There is however another possibility of escaping death. If a player, other than the victim, holds both jokers — those wild cards of Fortune — in one hand, they may be displayed at the last moment before the hanging. The game is then declared void and the victim is reprieved.

Murderers

Only confessed murderers are admitted to a scaffold. Membership is permanent and quarterly games mandatory for all members. As a new murderer in the walk, you survey the faces of the established population with scorn. 'I shall never become like them,' you tell yourself, as you stroll down the street, studying the apathy, the suppressed desperation. Yet, gradually, over the course of time your contempt dissolves into that same desperation. Inside you, the ghost of your victim begins its slow, insidious possession of your soul. You may relive, time and time again, those moments when you killed, especially if your victim was a former loved one. If you are without guilt, there is the bitterness of discovery and consequent flight. Eventually you sink into the same morass as your fellow malefactors and are drawn into the game out of despair.

Play

You begin the walk along the narrow street to your first game. Eventually you arrive at the inn where you are to play for your life. The faces of the other players register vague anticipation. The cards are dealt. The faces turn to stone.

You play the game perhaps once a quarter at first—then more frequently as the drug takes hold. As one of the eight winners, you feel the exhilaration of defeating the spectre of death. The group changes as new members are taken on in place of those who have drawn the death card. The more you win, the more you come to believe in a charmed existence, a superior destiny fashioned partly from luck and partly from the essential ingredient of a special *self*. You are not like the others. You move on a higher plane, god-like in your ability to thwart the noose.

Time

But eventually there comes a time when you draw the death card. At first the ace fails to register. It is tucked partly behind an innocent card. Then, suddenly, you see it. Inside you a silent scream begins. All the moisture leaves your mouth and your brains ferments with terror. You are sure all the other members know already, for how can such inner turmoil not show on your face? You put your own cards in your pocket, managing a smile, and call for a round of drinks. Then you slip away, after the first sip of ale, which tastes like vinegar, out into the night air. You begin running. You run north along the street, pausing only to puke. You run to the edge of the city-state, where the border guards of the neighbouring country stand ready. You turn and run in the opposite direction, to find them waiting there too. Then east. Then west. Finally, you trudge back to your lodgings in order to think, to formulate plans.

Twenty-four hours

There is only thing worse than not knowing when you are going to die—that is, *knowing*. You sit on the edge of your bed and stare around your room. You envy the cockroach that moves across the floor: you envy its lack of imagination. One minute your hands are dry, the next, damp. The weight of guilt has gone. You are about to atone. You try to tell yourself that what you feel is remorse, but you know that it is only regret for the deed that cannot be undone, the act that placed you in this uncompromising position. Your head turns over a thousand thoughts, but none of them lead to escape. Suddenly you understand why this sanctuary exists. It is a prison as secure as any with high walls and guards. In Murderers Walk, the prisoners try each other, and sentence each other to death.

Death

You wonder what the feel of the rope will be like against your neck. You touch your throat with your fingers. Will the spine break or will you expire slowly? Perhaps your lungs will burst? You try to imagine the pallor of your distended face: purple perhaps? Your eyes, huge balls easing out of their sockets? Your tongue hanging long between blue lips? You weep. Your mind goes numb. Your eyes are dry. Your head is full of a thousand active thoughts, each one a nightmare.

Void game

There is of course the possibility of a void game. It is not so unusual. But the closer the time comes, the surer you are that you will not be granted a reprieve. You have taken life and deserve no mercy. The hours pass quickly, and slowly; time races and stands still, depending on whether it is the pain of life, or death, that occupies you. One thing you are sure of: you cannot hope.

Absence

It is three minutes to the appointed hour. The other players will gather together with their cards. They will know, of course, by your absence, that you are the victim. They will be feeling high, victorious, excited. They will be talking in quick voices. Their eyes will be bright.

Eight am

You drag the chair beneath the beam as the others arrive. You hear their feet on the wooden stairs. These are sounds to treasure: every creak, every hollow footfall. They open the door and enter. Their faces are as ashen as yours had been on witnessing other deaths. The elation has been put aside for the moment. But it has to be done, for without a death there is no game, and without the game there is no life. This is as much an ordeal for them as it is for you—only the standpoint is different.

One of them hands you the rope. You stand on the chair hoping your legs will support you for just a few moments longer. You tie the rope to the beam. Your hands are unsteady. *Then—suddenly—you are ready to die.* In that moment all the terror has gone. You may still tremble, or wince, or blanch, but you are *ready.* It is not the moment of death that is so terrible, it is the preparation leading up to that moment. You are ready. You are ready. Just a moment longer…

End

One of the party steps forward and waves two jokers in your face. 'Void game,' he cries. 'You live to play again.' They pull you from the chair and jostle you towards the door, down the stairs and out into the street. Inside you the fear erupts again, and that precious moment, the moment when you were ready to die, has gone. They have stolen your death from you and you know you cannot retrieve that state of mind again, without reliving another twenty-four hours of terror.

That is when you dig your heels into the unyielding cobbles and grip a passing windowsill with fingers that would squeeze a rock to powder. That is when your mind flies open like a sprung trapdoor. That is when they drag you along the street, kicking and screaming, like a man being led to his execution.

ROSEMARY TIMPERLEY

Christmas Meeting

I have never spent Christmas alone before.

It gives me an uncanny feeling, sitting alone in my 'furnished room,' with my head full of ghosts, and the room full of voices of the past. It's a drowning feeling—all the Christmases of the past coming back in a mad jumble: the childish Christmas, with a house full of relations, a tree in the window, sixpences in the pudding, and the delicious, crinkly stocking in the dark morning; the adolescent Christmas, with mother and father, the War and the bitter cold, and the letters from abroad; the first really grown-up Christmas, with a lover—the snow and the enchantment, red wine and kisses, and the walk in the dark before midnight, with the grounds so white, and the stars diamond bright in a black sky—so many Christmases through the years.

And, now, the first Christmas alone.

But not quite loneliness. A feeling of companionship with all the other people who are spending Christmas alone—millions of them—past and present. A feeling that, if I close my eyes, there will be no past or future, only an endless present which *is* time, because it is all we ever have.

Yes, however cynical you are, however irreligious, it makes you feel queer to be alone at Christmas time.

So I'm absurdly relieved when the young man walks in. There's nothing romantic about it—I'm a woman of nearly fifty, a spinster schoolma'am with grim, dark hair, and myopic eyes that once were beautiful, and he's a kid of twenty, rather unconventionally dressed with a flowing, wine-coloured tie and black velvet jacket, and brown curls which could do with a taste of the barber's scissors. The effeminacy of his dress is belied by his features—narrow, piercing, blue eyes, and arrogant, jutting nose and chin. Not that he looks strong. The skin is fine-drawn over the prominent features,

81

and he is very white.

He bursts in without knocking, then pauses, says: 'I'm so sorry. I thought this was my room.' He begins to go out, then hesitates and says: 'Are you alone?'

'Yes.'

'It's—queer, being alone at Christmas, isn't it? May I stay and talk?'

'I'd be glad if you would.'

He comes right in, and sits down by the fire.

'I hope you don't think I came in here on purpose. I really did think it was my room.' he explains.

'I'm glad you made the mistake. But you're a very young person to be alone at Christmas time.'

'I wouldn't go back to the country to my family. It would hold up my work, I'm a writer.'

'I see.' I can't help smiling a little. That explains his rather unusual dress. And he takes himself so seriously, this young man! 'Of course, you mustn't waste a precious moment of writing,' I say with a twinkle.

'No, not a moment! That's what my family won't see. They don't appreciate urgency.'

'Families are never appreciative of the artistic nature.'

'No, they aren't,' he agrees seriously.

'What are you writing?'

'Poetry and a diary combined. It's called *My Poems and I,* by Francis Randel. That's my name. My family say there's no point in my writing, that I'm too young. But I don't feel young. Sometimes I feel like an old man, with too much to do before he dies.'

'Revolving faster and faster on the wheel of creativeness.'

'Yes! Yes, exactly! You understand! You must read my work some time. Please read my work! Read my work!' A note of desperation in his voice, a look of fear in his eyes, makes me say:

'We're both getting much to solemn for Christmas Day. I'm going to make you some coffee. And I have a plum cake.'

I move about, clattering cups, spooning coffee into my percolator. But I must have offended him, for, when I look round, I find he has left me. I am absurdly disappointed.

I finish making coffee, however, then turn to the bookshelf in the room. It is piled high with volumes, for which the landlady has apologised profusely: 'Hope you don't mind the books, Miss, but my husband won't part with them, and there's nowhere else to put them. We charge a bit less for the room for that reason.'

'I don't mind,' I said. 'Books are good friends.'

But these aren't very friendly-looking books. I take one at random. Or does some strange fate guide my hand?

Sipping my coffee, inhaling my cigarette smoke, I begin to read the battered little book, published, I see, in Spring, 1852. It's mainly poetry—immature stuff, but vivid. Then there's a kind of diary. More realistic, less affected. Out of curiosity, to see if there are any amusing comparisons, I turn to the entry for Christmas Day, 1851. I read:

'My first Christmas Day alone. I had rather an odd experience. When I went back to my lodgings after a walk, there was a middle-aged woman in my room. I thought, at first, I'd walked into the wrong room, but this was not so, and later, after a pleasant talk, she—disappeared. I suppose she was a ghost. But I wasn't frightened. I liked her. But I do not feel well to-night. Not at all well. I have never felt ill at Christmas before.'

A publisher's note followed the last entry:

Francis Randel died from a sudden heart attack on the night of Christmas Day, 1851. The woman mentioned in this final entry in his diary was the last person to see him alive. In spite of requests for her to come forward, she never did so. Her identity remains a mystery.

DYLAN THOMAS

J *arleys*

On the day that the travelling waxworks came to town the
attendant vanished. Next morning the proprietor called at the
employment agency and asked for a smart lad who could talk
English. But the smart lads talked Welsh, and the boy from
Bristol had a harelip. So the proprietor returned to his lodgings and, passing the canal, saw Eleazar reading on the bank.

'Any luck?' he enquired.

'I'm not fishing,' replied Eleazar.

He was immediately engaged.

It was late in the evening, and the last curious visitor had left
the tent. The proprietor counted the day's takings and went
away leaving Eleazar alone in the dark, wax world. Eleazar
removed the last cigarette-end from the ground, and brought
out a duster from his pocket. Tremblingly he dusted over the
lean, brown body of Hiawatha; tremblingly he patted the pale
cheeks of Charlie Peace; tremblingly he dusted over the wax
neck of Circe.

'You forgot my left calf,' said Hiawatha.

'You forgot my top lip,' said Charlie Peace.

'You forgot my right shoulder,' said the temptress.

Eleazar looked at the wax figures in amazement.

'You heard me', said Hiawatha.

'You heard me,' said Charlie Peace.

'You heard me,' said the temptress.

Eleazar stared around him. The entrance to the tent was a
long way off. There was no escape.

'Calf,' said Hiawatha.

'Lip,' said Charlie Peace.

'Shoulder,' said Circe.

Tremblingly Eleazar dusted over the strong-muscled calf;
tremblingly he patted the snarling lip; tremblingly he dusted

84

over the wax shoulder.

'That is certainly better,' said Hiawatha. 'You see,' he continued in apology, 'I used to run a lot; and you want your calves dusted then, don't you?'

'I do a lot of snarling,' said Charlie Peace.

'I do a lot of tempting,' said the temptress; 'though, really, I should be losing my fascination by this time; and my shoulder is not all that it was. I had it bitten in Aberdare once.'

'I remember the night well,' said Hiawatha. 'Somebody put an old hat on me.'

'I remember the night,' remarked the murderer, 'when as a child I stuck a needle into my nurse: it was a darning needle.'

'I remember chasing Minnehaha all over the rapids,' said Hiawatha. ' She used to be terribly annoyed when I called her Laughing Water.'

'I remember the sea-green eyes of Jason,' said Circe.

Eleazar could remember nothing. His first fears had vanished to be replaced by a sense of friendly curiosity. He inquired politely if all was well in the state of wax.

'Indeed,' said Hiawatha, 'I have little to complain of. There is a great deal to be said for being wax. One has few troubles. It is difficult to receive injury. The sharpest arrow could do little to me: a momentary impression soon to be filled in with a farthing's worth of wax from the local stores. It is a perpetual source of wonder to me that more people do not realise the advantages of a wax life.'

'How is it with you, ma'am?' asked Eleazar.

'There is still the desire to tempt,' replied the temptress, 'that I cannot conquer. And I still remember those confounded sea-green eyes.'

'Murder as a profession,' began Charlie Peace...

'Henry Wadsworth,' began Hiawatha...

'The history of temptation,' began the temptress...

And suddenly the three wax figures were still.

Eleazar shuffled further along the tent.

'Eleazar,' said an ape.

'Sir?' said Eleazar.

'Life,' said the ape, 'is a never-ending mystery. We are born. Why are we born? We die. The reason is obvious. The life of the body is short, and the veins are incapable of holding an eternal supply of blood.'

Eleazar would have continued on his way, but the ape held up its hand. 'Stop,' said the ape. 'Consider the man of flesh and the man of wax. Everything is done for the wax man; he is made painlessly and skilfully; he is found a house in a nice waterproof tent or in the interior of a large and hygienic building; he is clothed, brushed and dusted; he is the cynosure of all eyes. Think of the opportunities he enjoys to study the mentality of his near neighbour-man. Day after day, the faces of men are pressed close to mine; I see into men's eyes; I listen to their conversations. The man of wax is an unchanging, unprejudiced and unemotional observer of the human comedy.'

'Sir,' said Eleazar, 'you talk very well for an ape.'

'Eleazar,' said the ape, 'I have known this frame of wax for two days only. I was the late attendant.'

'Tell me,' said Eleazar, 'do you feel the cold?'

'Neither cold nor warmth.'

'Do you feel hunger?'

'Neither hunger nor thirst. I feel nothing. I want nothing. I am perpetually happy.'

Eleazar removed his jacket and trousers.

'Make room—move up,' said Eleazar.

Next morning the proprietor called at the employment agency, and asked for a smart lad.

'He must be careful, too,' he explained, 'for my waxworks has just been presented with an expensive new figure.'

'An historical figure?'

'No, no,' said the proprietor, 'the figure of a Welsh Druid in a long white shirt.'

PATRICIA MILES

Exit

'Come on,' said Hawkins eagerly, in his piping voice. 'Let's get off at the Post Office. We can soon walk up there.'

'In this?'

Carter gazed out doubtfully, as the bus rocketed along the empty road. Every now and then a few fat drops of rain fell out of a yellowish sky and dashed against the window. Beyond the hedges the fields, caught in the strange light, showed a living, incandescent green.

'Go on, be a sport. Come with me, will you? This is practically *ideal*.'

It wasn't the sort of weather most people would have called ideal. The storm had been brewing all day, with thunder rolling in the distance. What Hawkins meant was 'ideal for him', ie. ideal for trying out his theory.

'Come on,' said Hawkins again, getting agitated, 'we're nearly there.'

'Oh, all right,' Carter said then, out of good nature.

They grabbed up their school bags and Hawkins rang the bell. The bus stop served a few cottages and a farm a little way up the hill. One of the cottages was also a Post Office. Opposite the Post Office a track led up a gentle slope to a ruined chapel—their destination.

They crossed the road—there was hardly ever any traffic—and set off up the hill, rather clumsy and heavy-footed on the stones of the muddy path. They were laughing and larking about as they walked along.

'What exactly are you hoping to see?' said Carter. 'If hoping is the right word.'

'I'm not sure. Monks, white ladies, something like that.'

'What about the old nameless dread, eh?'

'That too.'

The path narrowed and they got into single file. They hadn't

87

far to go. The chapel was only a field or two away from the road, in a small wood fenced off—inadequately — with barbed wire. You could actually see the decayed end wall from the bus, if you looked at the right moment. All the same, close to civilization though it was, it had somehow succeeded in keeping its own peculiar atmosphere.

To his surprise, Carter found his mood changing: all his jokiness was dropping away: a feeling of oppression sat heavily in his chest. He wasn't going to let on to Hawkins, though. He decided it must be the weather. It was the queerest weather, so heavy and overcast. Thunder rumbled again. It was getting nearer.

'Listen to that!' continued his friend, still in the same loud tones. 'We should see something. Or it could be we'll just feel a drop in the temperature.'

Carter wished he'd let him come on his own. There wasn't all that much of a friendship between them: they just travelled in the same direction from school, and usually caught the same bus home. They weren't even in the same year. Hawkins was a clever little squirt out of Form Two, all specs and long words. Carter was older and brawnier. When they sat on the bus together Hawkins liked to rattle on, and Carter, who was good-natured, let him. He wasn't much of a talker himself. Hawkins was always full of ideas.

'Tell me it again,' said Carter, out of a dryish throat, 'your idea.'

They were nearly at the wood.

'It's simple, really', piped Hawkins, importantly. It wasn't simple at all, except at the start. 'My theory is, there is some connection between thunderstorms and psychic phenomena. You know that photograph I showed you out of the library— that one with the ghostly shape on it? That was taken at Corfe Castle just before a thunderstorm.'

'Bet it was a fake.'

'Maybe,' said Hawkins with scientific open-mindedness.

'And anyway—it wasn't taken here.'

'No, but it was in this sort of place, a well-known spooky spot. Even if that one was a fake, it doesn't really matter. The point is, there are so many accounts of apparitions and hauntings connected with storms, there must be something in it.'

'I wouldn't have thought you believed in ghosts.'

Hawkins shrugged. 'Well, I don't believe in ghosts, exactly. What I really think is, *either* something in the past leaves a sort of photograph, or film of itself, quite by accident, which you can pick up when the atmosphere's right; *or*—this is my other theory'—he paused impressively—'beings *from other worlds* reach through to us here. Whichever it is, it's connected with these special places, and storms.'

'*Other worlds?*'

'Yes. You know, out of deep space, or another time—what do you call it—an alternative universe. You see, if people here happened to see something like that, they'd naturally interpret it as a ghost, or the devil, or something supernatural, wouldn't they?'

Carter stood still, apparently to get his breath. 'You mean *we* might see things from outer space.'

'Lots of people have—UFOs and all that—they're always seeing them in Wales. Or we might see a funny sort of historical film, if my first theory's correct. Boy! If there is anything here, this is the day to see it.' He hurried eagerly up the last few yards of the path. Carter followed, slowly.

'Hawkins, what are you *supposed* to see here?'

'Dunno. I just know that it has this reputation for being haunted.'

It was easy getting into the wood. The wire had rusted through in places. There was a strong scent of bluebells everywhere; they were almost over, dying mostly. You couldn't walk without treading on them.

'Nothing stirring yet,' said Hawkins. In the wood even he sounded subdued, as if he had suddenly realised what in fact he might see. Carter moved his shoulders uneasily: it was a curious animal uneasiness, purely physical. He had not believed a word Hawkins had said.

They went on towards the chapel. Most of its grey stones had been carted away years ago, but the foundations and one wall remained. The thunder sounded again, but it seemed further off now.

'Well, this is it.' There was a quaver in Hawkins's voice, and he jumped when a spatter of rain fell on him. A raindrop ran like a tear down his glasses. And then he disappeared.

Suddenly, and with great completeness, Hawkins was no longer there. Carter had been staring right at him, even noticing the yellow streak of light reflected in his glasses and the splosh of rain. The light had touched the wall too, just above his friend's head.

Wait. It was at this point that the blood in Carter's veins chilled to ice water, and that each hair rose separately on his head and arms.

There was *no wall*. He turned round. There were no trees, no electric pylons, no cottages, no road. The lie of the land was not the same. There was no storm. The sky was clear, a curious pale mauve colour. There was no sun. He was standing alone in a rocky place, and a small wind was blowing. A wild facetiousness swept over him. He started to laugh. *He* was the one who had disappeared. Exit. Finis. Out goes he.

Then he burst into tears. 'That Hawkins, when I get hold of him, I'll kill him. I'll duff him up. I'll make him wish he'd never been born.'

Of course, he was never able to do any of these things.

JULIA O'FAOLAIN

Legend for a Painting

A knight rode to a place where a lady was living with a dragon. She was a gently bred creature with a high forehead, and her dress—allowing for her surroundings—was neat. While the dragon slept, the knight had a chance to present himself.

'I have come,' he told the lady, 'to set you free.' He pointed at a stout chain linking her to her monstrous companion. It had a greenish tinge, due the knight supposed to some canker oozing from the creature's flesh.

Green was the dragon's colour. Its tail was green; so were its wings, with the exception of the pale pink eyes which were embedded in them and which glowed like water-lilies and expanded when the dragon flew, as eyes do on the spread tails of peacocks. Greenest of all was the dragon's under-belly which swelled like sod on a fresh grave. It was heaving just now and emitting gurgles. The knight shuddered.

'What,' the lady wondered, 'do you mean by "free"?'

The knight spelled it: 'F-R-E-E', although he was unsure whether or not she might be literate. 'To go!' he gasped for he was grappling with distress.

'But where?' the lady insisted. 'I like it here, you know. Draggie and I'—the knight feared her grin might be mischievous or even mad—'have a perfect symbiotic relationship!'

The knight guessed at obscenities.

'I clean his scales,' she said, 'and he prepares my food. We have no cutlery so he chews it while it cooks in the fire from his throat: a labour-saving device. He can do rabbit stew, braised wood-pigeon, even liver Venetian style when we can get a liver.'

'God's blood!' the knight managed to swear. His breath had been taken away.

'I don't know that recipe. Is it good? I can see,' the lady wisely soothed, 'you don't approve. But remember that fire scours. His mouth is germ free. Cleaner than mine or your own, which, if I may say so with respect, has been breathing too close. Have you perhaps been chewing wild garlic?'

The knight crossed himself. 'You,' he told the lady, 'must be losing your wits as a result of living with this carnal beast!' He sprinkled her with a little sacred dust from a pouch that he carried about his person. He had gathered it on the grave of Saint George the Dragon Killer and trusted in its curative properties. 'God grant,' he prayed, 'you don't lose your soul as well. Haven't you heard that if a single drop of dragon's blood falls on the mildest man or maid, they grow as carnal as the beast itself? Concupiscent!' he hissed persuasively. 'Bloody! Fierce!'

The lady sighed. 'Blood does obsess you!' she remarked. 'Draggie never bleeds. You needn't worry. His skin's prime quality. Very resistant and I care for him well. He may be "carnal" as you say. We're certainly both carnivores. I take it you're a vegetarian?'

The knight glanced at the cankered chain and groaned. 'You're mad!' he ground his teeth. 'Your sense of values has been perverted. The fact that you can't see it proves it!'

'A tautology, I think?' The lady grinned. 'Why don't you have a talk with old Draggie when he wakes up? You'll see how gentle he can be. That might dispel your prejudices.'

But the knight had heard enough. He neither liked long words nor thought them proper in a woman's mouth. *Deeds not words* was the motto emblazoned on his shield, for he liked words that condemned words and this, as the lady could have told him, revealed inner contradications likely to lead to trouble in the long run.

'Enough!' he yelled and, lifting his lance, plunged it several times between the dragon's scales. He had no difficulty in doing this, for the dragon was a slow-witted, somnolent beast at best and just now deep in a private dragon-dream. Its eyes, when they opened, were iridescent and flamed in the sunlight, turning, when the creature wept, into great, concentric, rainbow wheels of fire. 'Take that!' the knight was howling gleefully, 'and that and that!'

Blood spurted, gushed, and spattered until his face, his polished armour and the white coat of his charger were veined and flecked like porphyry. The dragon was soon dead but the knight's rage seemed unstoppable. For minutes, as though battening on its own release, it continued to discharge as he hacked at the unresisting carcass. Butchering, his sword swirled and slammed. His teeth gnashed. Saliva flowed in stringy beardlets from his chin and the lady stared at him in horror. She had been pale before but now her cheeks seemed to have gathered sour, greenish reflections into their brimming hollows.

Abruptly, she dropped the chain. Its clank, as it hit a stone, interrupted the knight's frenzy. As though just awakened, he turned dull eyes to her. Questioning.

'Then,' slowly grasping what this meant, 'you were never his prisoner, after all?'

The lady pointed at a gold collar encircling the dragon's neck. It had been concealed by an overlap of scales but had slipped into view during the fight. One end of the chain was fastened to it.

'He was mine,' she said. 'But as I told you he was gentle and more a pet than a prisoner.'

The knights wiped his eyelids which were fringed with red. He looked at his hands.

'Blood!' he shrieked. 'Dragon's blood!'

'Yes,' she said in a cold, taut voice, 'you're bloody. Concupiscent, no doubt? Fierce, certainly! Carnal?' She kicked the chain, which had broken when she threw it down and, bending, picked up a link that had become detached. 'I'll wear this,' she said bitterly, 'in token of my servitude. I'm your prisoner now.' She slipped the gold, green-tinged metal ring on to the third finger of her left hand. It too was stained with blood.

D*rought*

Whirling pillars of dust walk the brown floor of the earth. Trembling, the roots of the withered grass await the rain; thirsty for green love the vast and arid plain treks endlessly out to its horizon. One straight ruler-laid railway track shoots from under the midday sun's glare towards where a night will be velvet-cool with stars. The landscape is that of drought. Tiny as two grains of sand, a white man and a black man build a wall. Four walls. Then a roof. A house.

The black man carries blocks of stone and the white man lays them in place. The white man stands inside the walls where there is some shade. He says: 'You must work outside. You have a black skin, you can stand the sun better than I can.'

The black man laughs at his muscles glistening in the sun. A hundred years ago his ancestors reaped dark harvests with their assegais, and threshed out the fever of the black sun in their limbs with the Ngoma-dance. Now the black man laughs while he begins to frown.

'Why do you always talk of my black skin?' he asks.

'You are cursed,' the white man says. 'Long ago my God cursed you with darkness.'

'Your God is white,' the black man angrily replies. 'Your God lies! I love the sun and I fear the dark.'

The white man speaks dreamily on: 'Long ago my forefathers came across the sea. Far they came, in white ships tall as trees, and on the land they built them waggons and covered them with the sails of their ships. Far they travelled and spread their campfire ashes over this vast barbaric land. But now their children are tired, we want to build houses and teach you blacks how to live in peace with us. It is time, even if your skins will always be black...'

Proudly the black man counters: 'And my ancestors dipped the assegais in the blood of your forefathers and saw that it

94

was red as blood. Red as the blood of the impala that our young men run to catch between the two red suns of the hills!'

'It's time you forgot the damned past,' the white man sadly says. 'Come, you must learn to work with me. We must build this house.'

'You come to teach me that God is white. That I should build a house for the white man.' The black man stands with folded arms.

'Kaffir!' the white man shouts, 'will you never understand anything at all! Do what I tell you!'

'Yes, Baas,' the black man mutters.

The black man carries blocks of stone and the white man lays them in place. He makes the walls strong. The sun glares down with its terrible eye. Far, as the only tree in the parched land, a pillar of dust walks the trembling horizon.

'This damned heat!' the white man mutters, 'if only it would rain.'

Irritably he wipes the sweat from his forehead before he says: 'Your ancestors are dead. It's time you forgot them.'

Silently the black man looks at him with eyes that answer: Your ancestors, too, are dead. We are alone here.

Alone in the dry and empty plain the white man and the black man build a house. They do not speak to each other. They build the four walls and then the roof. The black man works outside in the sun and the white man inside in the shade. Now the black man can only see the white man's head. They lay the roof.

'Baas,' the black man asks at last, 'why has your house no windows and no doors?'

The white man has become very sad. 'That, too, you cannot understand,' he says. 'Long ago in another country my forefathers built walls to keep out the sea. Thick, watertight walls. That's why my house, too, has no windows and no doors.'

'But there's no big water here!' the black man exclaims, 'the sand is dry as a scull!'

You're the sea, the white man thinks, but it too sad to explain.

They lay the roof. They nail the last plank, the last

corrugated iron sheet, the black man outside and the white man inside. Then the black man can see the white man no more.

'Baas!' he calls, but hears no answer.

The Inkoos cannot get out, he thinks with fright, he cannot see the sky or know when it is day or night. The Inkoos will die inside his house!

The black man hammers with his fists on the house and calls: 'But Baas, no big water will ever come here! Here it will never rain forty days and forty nights as the Book of your white God says!'

He hears no answer and he shouts: 'Come out, Baas!'

He hears no answer.

With his fists still raised as if to knock again, the black man raises his eyes bewilderedly to the sky empty of a single cloud, and stares around him at the horizon where red-hot pillars of dust dance the fearful Ngoma of the drought.

Alone and afraid, the black man stammers: 'Come out, Baas... Come out to me...'

Elethia

A certain perverse experience shaped Elethia's life, and made it possible for it to be true that she carried with her at all times a small apothecary jar of ashes.

There was in the town where she was born a man whose ancestors had owned a large plantation on which everything under the sun was made or grown. There had been many slaves, and though slavery no longer existed, this grandson of former slave-owners held a quaint proprietary point of view where coloured people were concerned. He adored them, of course. Not in the present—it went without saying—but at that time, stopped, just on the outskirts of his memory: his grandfather's time.

This man, whom Elethia never saw, opened a locally famous restaurant on a busy street near the centre of town. He called it 'Old Uncle Albert's.' In the window of the restaurant was a stuffed likeness of Uncle Albert himself, a small brown dummy of waxen skin and glittery black eyes. His lips were intensely smiling and his false teeth shone. He carried a covered tray in one hand, raised level with his shoulder, and over his other arm was draped a white napkin.

Black people could not eat at Uncle Albert's, though they worked, of course, in the kitchen. But on Saturday afternoons a crowd of them would gather to look at 'Uncle Albert' and discuss how near to the real person the dummy looked. Only the very old people remembered Albert Porter, and their eyesight was no better than their memory. Still there was comfort somehow in knowing that Albert's likeness was here before them daily and that if he smiled as a dummy in a fashion he was not known to do as a man, well, perhaps both memory and eyesight were wrong.

The old people appeared grateful to the rich man who owned the restaurant for giving them a taste of vicarious fame.

They could pass by the gleaming window where Uncle Albert stood, seemingly in the act of sprinting forward with his tray, and know that though niggers were not allowed in the front door, ole Albert was already inside, and looking mighty pleased about it, too.

For Elethia the fascination was in Uncle Albert's finger-nails. She wondered how his creator had got them on. She wondered also about the white hair that shone so brightly under the lights. One summer she worked as a salad girl in the restaurant's kitchen, and it was she who discovered the truth about Uncle Albert. He was not a dummy; he was stuffed. Like a bird, like a moose's head, like a giant bass. He was stuffed.

One night after the restaurant was closed someone broke in and stole nothing but Uncle Albert. It was Elethia and her friends, boys who were in her class and who called her 'Thia'. Boys who bought Thunderbird and shared it with her. Boys who laughed at her jokes so much they hardly remembered she was also cute. Her tight buddies. They carefully burned Uncle Albert to ashes in the incinerator of their high school, and each of them kept a bottle of his ashes. And for each of them what they knew and their reaction to what they knew was profound.

The experience undercut whatever solid foundation Elethia had assumed she had. She became secretive, wary, looking over her shoulder at the slightest noise. She haunted the museums of any city in which she found herself, looking, usually, at the remains of Indians, for they were plentiful everywhere she went. She discovered some of the Indian warriors and maidens in the museums were also real, stuffed people, painted and wigged and robed, like figures in the Rue Morgue. There were so many, in fact, that she could not possibly steal and burn them all. Besides, she did not know if these figures—with their valiant glass eyes—would wish to be burned.

About Uncle Albert she felt she knew...

What kind of man was Uncle Albert?

Well, the old folks said, he wasn't nobody's uncle and wouldn't sit still for nobody to call him that, either.

Why, said another old-timer, I recalls the time they hung a

boy's privates on a post at the end of the street where all the black folks shopped, just to scare us all, you understand, and Albert Porter was the one took 'em down and buried 'em. Us never did find the rest of the boy though. It was just like always—they would throw you in the river with a big old green log tied to you, and down to the bottom you sunk.

He continued:

Albert was born in slavery and he remembered that his mamma and daddy didn't know nothing about slavery'd done ended for near 'bout ten years, the boss man kept them so ignorant of the law, you understand. So he was a mad so-an'-so when he found out. They used to beat him severe trying to make him forget the past and grin and act like a nigger. (Whenever you saw somebody acting like a nigger, Albert said, you could be sure he seriously disremembered his past.) But he never would. Never would work in the big house as head servant, neither—always broke up stuff. The master at that time was always going around pinching him too. Looks like he hated Albert more than anything—but he never would let him get a job anywhere else. And Albert never would leave home. Too stubborn.

Stubborn, yes. My land, another one said. That's why it do seem strange to see that dummy that sposed to be ole Albert with his mouth open. All them teeth. Hell, all Albert's teeth was knocked out before he was grown...

Elethia went away to college and her friends went into the army because they were poor and that was the way things were. They discovered Uncle Alberts all over the world. Elethia was especially disheartened to find Uncle Alberts in her textbooks, in the newspapers and on TV.

Everywhere she looked there was an Uncle Albert (and many Aunt Albertas, it goes without saying).

But she had her jar of ashes, the old-timers' memories written down, and her friends who wrote that in the army they were learning skills that would get them through more than a plate glass window.

And she was careful that, no matter how compelling the hype, Uncle Alberts, in her own mind, were not permitted to exist.

OLIVE SCHREINER

The Woman's Rose

I have an old, brown, carved box; the lid is broken and tied with a string. In it I keep little squares of paper, with hair inside, and a little picture which hung over my brother's bed when we were children, and other things as small. I have in it a rose. Other women also have such boxes where they keep such trifles, but no one has my rose.

When my eye is dim, and my heart grows faint, and my faith in woman flickers, and her present is an agony to me, and her future a despair, the scent of that dead rose, withered for twelve years, comes back to me. I know there will be spring; as surely as the birds know it when they see above the snow two tiny, quivering green leaves. Spring cannot fail us.

There were other flowers in the box once: a bunch of white acacia flowers, gathered by the strong hand of a man, as we passed down a village street on a sultry afternoon, when it had rained, and the drops fell on us from the leaves of the acacia trees. The flowers were damp; they made mildew marks on the paper I folded them in. After many years I threw them away. There is nothing of them left in the box now, but a faint, strong smell of dried acacia, that recalls that sultry summer afternoon; but the rose is in the box still.

It is many years ago now; I was a girl of fifteen, and I went to visit in a small up-country town. It was young in those days, and two days' journey from the nearest village; the population consisted mainly of men. A few were married, and had their wives and children, but most were single. There was only one young girl there when I came. She was about seventeen, fair, and rather fully-fleshed; she had large dreamy blue eyes, and wavy light hair; full, rather heavy lips, until she smiled; then her face broke into dimples, and all her white teeth shone. The hotel-keeper may have had a daughter, and the farmer in the outskirts had two, but we never saw them. She reigned alone. All the men worshipped her. She was the only woman they had to think of. They talked of her on the 'stoep', at the market, at the hotel; they watched for her at street corners; they hated the man she bowed to or walked with down the street. They brought flowers to the front door; they offered her their horses; they begged her to marry them when they dared. Partly, there was something noble and heroic in this devotion of men to the best woman they knew; partly there was something natural in it, that these men, shut off from the world, should pour at the feet of one woman the worship that otherwise would have been given to twenty; and partly there was something mean in their envy of one another. If she had raised her little finger, I suppose, she might have married any one out of twenty of them.

Then I came. I do not think I was prettier; I do not think I was so pretty as she was. I was certainly not as handsome. But I was vital, and I was new, and she was old—they all forsook her and followed me. They worshipped me. It was to my door that the flowers came; it was I had twenty horses offered me when I could only ride one; it was for me they waited at street corners; it was what I said and did that they talked of. Partly I liked it. I had lived alone all my life; no one ever had told me I was beautiful and a woman. I believed them. I did not know it was simply a fashion, which one man had set and the rest followed unreasoningly. I liked them to ask me to marry them, and to say, No. I despised them. The mother heart had not swelled in me yet; I do not know all men were my children, as the large woman knows when her heart is grown. I was too small to be tender. I liked my power. I was like a child with a new whip, which it goes about cracking everywhere, not caring against what. I could not wind it up and put it away. Men were curious creatures, who liked me, I could never tell why. Only one thing took from my pleasure; I could not bear that they had deserted her for me. I liked her great dreamy blue eyes, I liked her slow walk and drawl; when I saw her sitting among men, she seemed to me much too good to be among them; I would have given all their compliments if she would once have smiled at me as she smiled at them, with all her face breaking into radiance, with her dimples and flashing teeth. But I knew it never could be; I felt sure she hated me; that she wished I was dead; that she wished I had never come to the village. She did not know, when we went out riding, and a man who had always ridden beside her came to ride beside me, that I sent him away; that once when a man thought to win my favour by ridiculing her slow drawl before me I turned on him so fiercely that he never dared come before me again. I knew she knew that at the hotel men had made a bet as to which was the prettier, she or I, and had asked each man who came in, and that the one who had staked on me won. I hated them for it, but I would not let her see that I cared about what she felt towards me.

She and I never spoke to each other.

If we met in the village street we bowed and passed on; when we shook hands we did so silently, and did not look at each other. But I thought she felt my presence in a room just as I felt hers.

At last the time for my going came. I was to leave the next day. Someone I knew gave a party in my honour, to which all the village was invited.

It was midwinter. There was nothing in the gardens but a few dahlias and chrysanthemums, and I suppose that for two hundred miles round there was not a rose to be bought for love or money. Only in the garden of a friend of mine, in a sunny corner between the oven and brick wall, there was a rose tree growing which had on it one bud. It was white, and it had been promised to the fair-haired girl to wear at the party.

The evening came; when I arrived and went to the waiting-room, to take off my mantle, I found the girl there already. She was dressed in pure white, with her great white arms and shoulders showing, and her bright hair glittering in the candlelight, and the white rose fastened at her breast. She looked like a queen. I said 'Good-evening,' and turned away quickly to the glass to arrange my old black scarf across my old black dress.

Then I felt a hand touch my hair.

'Stand still,' she said.

I looked in the glass. She had taken the white rose from her breast, and was fastening it in my hair.

'How nice dark hair is; it sets off flowers so.' She stepped back and looked at me. 'It looks much better there!'

I turned round.

'You are so beautiful to me,' I said.

'Y-e-s,' she said, with her slow Colonial drawl; 'I'm so glad.'

We stood looking at each other.

Then they came in and swept us away to dance. All the evening we did not come near to each other. Only once, as she passed, she smiled at me.

The next morning I left the town.

I never saw her again.

Years afterwards I heard she had married and gone to America; it may or may not be so—but the rose—the rose is in the box still! When my faith in woman grows dim, and it seems that for want of love and magnanimity she can play no part in any future heaven; then the scent of that small withered thing comes back—spring cannot fail us.

ELSA JOUBERT

M*ilk*

The man with dust embedded in the grooves of his face spoke slowly. Occasionally he ran a hand over his head in an attempt to flatten his sparse hair. The interpreter followed on the heels of his words, and someone—a reporter?—scribbled them down.

The words were dragged out of him. They couldn't get enough. At intervals he swallowed hard; then continued:

He had pressed his pistol against my temple. How he had come to be beside me in the car, I do not know. By then they had already dragged my wife from the car. He had said: Move and you're dead.

I did not hear her scream—or utter any sound. Behind me— the seats were folded down—the children slept.

I sat still. What could I have done? The barrel of the pistol was biting into my skin. When the second one took the pistol, he had slid a hand over the other's, squeezing his body in next to mine while the other edged out.

There was not a moment in which the barrel was not pressed against my temple. I think five or six of them raped my wife.

When they were finished with her, they wanted to leave her alongside the road. But I would not drive without my wife. We were part of a long convoy of cars which had ground to a halt, and I was delaying it.

They wrenched the door open again and flung her back into the car. Her hair hung loose, her bloodied lips were swollen. Her eyes wore a strange expression.

She attempted to rearrange her torn clothes, for she was raised very correctly. All she said to me was: Drive.

When I switched on the ignition, the convoy also began to move. I inched forward in first gear. Later, when we picked up more speed, I was able to change to second and then to third gear. In the distance—and directly behind us—I could hear gunfire, but we were not stopped again.

When we reached the South African border post, there was little delay. A young soldier with clean fatigues and a clean-shaven face merely waved us by and said: Don't stop driving, go through.

They spent that night in an emergency camp.

The military tents billowed in the darkness, the cars turned into the dusty tracks between the tents or were parked in the veld against the wire. There the couple made a bed and attempted to sleep. They lay between the wire and the car, on a thin mattress allocated them by the soldiers.

Tears ran down his cheeks as his hands traversed her body. She swept greying hair from her damp forehead and talked quietly to the man: Try to come to terms with it. It is past.

He entered her torn body as a man would enter his house after a fire had ravaged it.

Did he wish to heal her?

Or was it fear that he spilled? Or doubt, or guilt?

He discovered her condition three months later. He gazed at her as though he were weighing something up and said: You're expecting a child?

And later he asked: Is it my child?

How can I know? she replied.

For as long as she could, she concealed it, here in the new cottage in the new township, in the new country. In the mornings when the children had left for their new school, the man to his new job, she gave herself over to nausea. It was a relief to be alone, to be able to lean over the bowl and allow the sickness to well up. The nausea persisted, her body deteriorated; the foetus clung to her spinal column like an alien growth.

He took her to the maternity home and filled in the forms, printed the name of his wife: Maria Margarida da Silva. His name, the name of his new medical fund, his religious denomination.

Because she was no longer young, they wheeled her in carefully.

The delivery was not that difficult. The body, which had nurtured the growing child for nine months, thrust it out with ease. With relief? And when the child was brought to the woman and she identified it and saw it resembled her other babies in skin and features, she wept.

The other women in the ward with her uttered comforting sounds: her weeping was natural. They recognised in her a stranger, fearful after flight. Allow the tears to fall. One woman raised herself on an elbow, and with her emptied belly resting heavily on the bed assured her: It's nature's way of getting rid of excess water, those tears.

Maria Margarida da Silva took the newborn child they brought her into the curve of her arm. She unbuttoned the nightdress and the blue-tinged lips closed greedily on the nipple and began to suck. She felt the tugging at her nipple and also how the moistness, not yet milk but mother-fluid which made the child still part of the mother-body, was painfully wrung from the reluctant nipple. She looked down and saw a hand grope free from its wrappings and stray blindly about until it encountered the soft swell of her breast and clamped to it. The fingers clawed so tightly that the flesh ballooned between them. The tugging at her nipple was so insistent that the nerve-ends throughout her body were aware of it.

Only on the second day did she examine the child closely. It resembled her other two children; only the lips were thicker, slightly more pursed—or was it merely craving for milk?—a little boy, even when covered and satiated in his blankets, still purses his mouth for milk. The nose, also, was different, but not noticeably so, and what baby's nose is fully formed? Are not noses all created as finger-marks in unworked clay?

The hand folded over her fingers with a convulsive grasp. The child was reluctant to release her, even when the smiling nurse attempted to unlock the little hand with her strong fingers.

Such a grip. The child would make his mark.

On the third day the small face peering from its covers showed a dark tint, as though a shadow had fallen over it. Maria da Silva glanced at the window, but the blind was not drawn. She looked at her own hand, which held the child in the crook of her arm, but the shadow had not fallen over her skin.

The child drank. It felt as if every swallow drained the life fluid from her marrow, her bones, from her deepest recesses. She attempted to tug the child from her breast, but the lips clung.

When the young nurse came to fetch the child, she handled him in a curious manner, as though she were keeping him at a distance—or, dear mother of God, was it her imagination that had created the impression? Was there revulsion for the baby in her eyes?

Her husband had visited her on the night of the second day.

He did not talk much about the child.

Things are going well, he said. The house is better than the one in Portugal, even the one in Angola. They are using me to the best of my ability at the factory. In the department I work in now, I know as much as the cleverest among them. And they know it. They need people with my training.

She was pleased by his confidence. She thought of the night when he had probed her wounds, when he had driven his guilt into her, when tears had coursed from his eyes.

Now his cheeks were clean and his hands lay still on the coverlet, or occasionally grasped her arm. He had brought flowers for her.

And the children? she asked.

They are well. The school helps them, even with the language.

That's good, she said. He ran a clumsy hand over her head, stroking flat the greying hair.

When the child was brought to her on the fourth day, the colour of his little face was grey, like ash, and in the armpits and the soft folds of his skin, black.

The nurse carried the child to her without a word, and laid it at her side. With the new black shadow that had spread over the skin, the structure of the nose was more apparent. It was wide, broad-flanged, like that of the man who had dragged her from the car, while her husband sat with the barrel of a pistol against his temple.

The child's mouth searched greedily for her breast, and

when he encountered the milkiness of the nipple it began to nibble, to search, to clutch. The first drops oozed, giving her immediate relief.

She held the child's nose between thumb and finger. The baby struggled. Who would have thought there was so much strength in the tiny body? The feet pounded in fury against her belly, the hands beat against her full breasts. The mouth left her nipple and fought for breath in open confusion. The milk he had been drinking ran in white beads from the corners of his mouth.

She pushed the blanket into his open mouth, and shoved it deeper and deeper.

She held it there until the kicking against her abdomen subsided, until the grip on her breast relaxed and the hands with dark-shadowed fingers fell away from her.

She rang and rang the bell until the nurse at last arrived; then she said: The child suffocated.

The reporter wanted a story. He approached Maria da Silva in the room. The nurse is my girlfriend, he said. She told me there's a story.

She gestured with a hand: I don't understand you.

He attempted to indicate: The child at your breast. . . did you fall asleep? He folded his hands together, held them at an angle, leant his head against them to mimic sleep. Did you fall asleep and smother the child beneath your breast?

She nods. She is tired.

The people want to know, the reporter urges. They take an interest. Tragedy in the new country.

Tears stream over the cheeks of the woman lying in the bed, the white coverlet pulled up to her chin over swollen breasts. The tears collect in the corners of her eyes. Unattractive eyes, for they are wrinkled and old and tired and her hair is streaked with grey. They collect in the corners of her eyes and run in rivulets down her cheeks. She does not wipe them away.

Her arms lie wide and brown and stocky on the coverlet. The streaked hank of hair lies at her left side, like a dead, dark animal beside her.

How does it feel to have smothered your baby? the reporter

asks. He is over-hasty, he fears that it will all come to nothing. I want a caption for the picture.

Then even he falls silent before the tears which flow from the woman's eyes, down her cheeks.

She gestures at her breasts. The moisture seeps through the nightdress.

What do I do with the milk? she asks wordlessly. Who do I feed with the milk?

Translated by Mark Swift

The Kiss

It was still quite light out of doors, but inside with the curtains drawn and the smouldering fire sending out a dim, uncertain glow, the room was full of deep shadows.

Brantain sat in one of these shadows; it had overtaken him and he did not mind. The obscurity lent him courage to keep his eyes fastened as ardently as he liked upon the girl who sat in the firelight.

She was very handsome, with a certain fine, rich colouring that belongs to the healthy brune type. She was quite composed, as she idly stroked the satiny coat of the cat that lay curled in her lap, and she occasionally sent a slow glance into the shadow where her companion sat. They were talking low, of indifferent things which plainly were not the things that occupied their thoughts. She knew that he loved her—a frank, blustering fellow without guile enough to conceal his feelings, and no desire to do so. For two weeks past he had sought her society eagerly and persistently. She was confidently waiting for him to declare himself and she meant to accept him. The rather insignificant and unattractive Brantain was enormously rich; and she liked and required the entourage which wealth could give her.

During one of the pauses between their talk of the last tea and the next reception the door opened and a young man entered whom Brantain knew quite well. The girl turned her face toward him. A stride or two brought him to her side, and bending over her chair—before she could suspect his intention, for she did not realise that he had not seen her visitor—he pressed an ardent, lingering kiss upon her lips.

Brantain slowly arose; so did the girl arise, but quickly, and the new-comer stood between them, a little amusement and some defiance struggling with the confusion in his face.

'I believe,' stammered Brantain, 'I see that I have stayed too long. I—I had no idea—that is, I must wish you good-by.' He was clutching his hat with both hands, and probably did not perceive that she was extending her hand to him, her presence of mind had not completely deserted her; but she could not have trusted herself to speak.

'Hang me if I saw him sitting there, Nattie! I know it's deuced awkward for you. But I hope you'll forgive me this once—this very first break. Why, what's the matter?'

'Don't touch me; don't come near me,' she returned angrily. 'What do you mean by entering the house without ringing?'

'I came in with your brother, as I often do,' he answered coldly, in self-justification. 'We came in the side way. He went upstairs and I came in here hoping to find you. The explanation is simple enough and ought to satisfy you that the misadventure was unavoidable. But do say that you forgive me, Nathalie,' he entreated, softening.

'Forgive you! You don't know what you are talking about. Let me pass. It depends upon—a good deal whether I ever forgive you.'

At that next reception which she and Brantain had been talking about she approached the young man with a delicious frankness of manner when she saw him there.

'Will you let me speak to you a moment or two, Mr Brantain?' she asked with an engaging but perturbed smile. He seemed extremely unhappy; but when she took his arm and walked away with him, seeking a retired corner, a ray of hope mingled with the almost comical misery of his expression. She was apparently very outspoken.

'Perhaps I should not have sought this interview, Mr Brantain; but—but, oh, I have been very uncomfortable, almost miserable since that little encounter the other afternoon. When I thought how you might have misinterpreted it, and believed things'—hope was plainly gaining the ascendancy over misery in Brantain's round, guileless face—'of course, I know it is nothing to you, but for my own sake I do want you to understand that Mr Harvy is an intimate friend of long standing. Why, we have always been like cousins—like brother and sister, I may say. He is my brother's most intimate associate and often fancies that he is entitled to the same privileges as the family. Oh, I know it is absurd, uncalled for, to tell you this; undignified even,' she was almost weeping, 'but it makes so much difference to me what you think of—of me.' Her voice had grown very low and agitated. The misery had all disappeared from Brantain's face.

'Then you do really care what I think, Miss Nathalie? May I call you Miss Nathalie?' They turned into a long, dim corridor that was lined on either side with tall, graceful plants. They walked slowly to the very end of it. When they turned to retrace their steps Brantain's face was radiant and hers was triumphant.

Harvy was among the guests at the wedding; and he sought her out in a rare moment when she stood alone.

'Your husband', he said, smiling, 'has sent me over to kiss you.'

A quick blush suffused her face and round polished throat. 'I suppose it's natural for a man to feel and act generously on an occasion of this kind. He tells me he doesn't want his marriage to interrupt wholly that pleasant intimacy which has existed between you and me. I don't know what you've been telling him,' with an insolent smile, 'but he has sent me here to kiss you.'

She felt like a chess player who, by the clever handling of his pieces, sees the game taking the course intended. Her eyes were bright and tender with a smile as they glanced up into his; and her lips looked hungry for the kiss which they invited.

'But, you know,' he went on quietly, 'I didn't tell him so, it would have seemed ungrateful, but I can tell you. I've stopped kissing women; it's dangerous.'

Well, she had Brantain and his million left. A person can't have everything in this world; and it was a little unreasonable of her to expect it.

The Breadwinner

The parents of a boy of fourteen were waiting for him to come home with his first week's wages.

The mother had laid the table and was cutting some slices of bread and butter for tea. She was a little woman with a pinched face and a spare body, dressed in a blue blouse and skirt, the front of the skirt covered with a starched white apron. She looked tired and frequently sighed heavily.

The father, sprawling inelegantly in an old armchair by the fireside, legs outstretched, was little too. He had watery blue eyes and a heavy brown moustache, which he sucked occasionally.

These people were plainly poor, for the room, though clean, was meanly furnished, and the thick pieces of bread and butter were the only food on the table.

As she prepared the meal, the woman from time to time looked contemptuously at her husband. He ignored her, raising his eyebrows, humming, or tapping his teeth now and then with his finger-nails, making a pretence of being profoundly bored.

'You'll keep your hands off the money,' said the woman, obviously repeating something that she had already said several times before. 'I know what'll happen to it if you get hold of it. He'll give it to me. It'll pay the rent and buy us a bit of food, and not go into the till at the nearest public-house.'

'You shut your mouth,' said the man, quietly.

'I'll not shut my mouth!' cried the woman, in a quick burst of anger. 'Why should I shut my mouth? You've been boss here for long enough. I put up with it when you were bringing money into the house, but I'll not put up with it now. You're nobody here. Understand? *Nobody*. I'm boss and he'll hand the money to me!'

'We'll see about that,' said the man, leisurely poking the fire.

Nothing more was said for about five minutes.

Then the boy came in. He did not look older then ten or eleven years. He looked absurd in long trousers. The whites of his eyes against his black face gave him a startled expression.

The father got to his feet.

'Where's the money?' he demanded.

The boy looked from one to the other. He was afraid of his father. He licked his pale lips.

'Come on now,' said the man. 'Where's the money?'

'Don't give it to him,' said the woman. 'Don't give it to him, Billy. Give it to me.'

The father advanced on the boy, his teeth showing in a snarl under his big moustache.

'Where's the money?' he almost whispered.

The boy looked him straight in the eyes.

'I lost it,' he said.

'You—*what*?' cried his father.

'I lost it,' the boy repeated.

The man began to shout and wave his hands about.

'Lost it! *Lost it!* What are you talking about? How could you lose it?'

'It was in a packet,' said the boy, 'a little envelope. I lost it.'

'Where did you lose it?'

'I don't know. I must have dropped it in the street.'

'Did you go back and look for it?'

The boy nodded. 'I couldn't find it,' he said.

The man made a noise in his throat, half grunt, half moan—the sort of noise that an animal would make.

'So you lost it, did you?' he said. He stepped back a couple of paces and took off his belt—a wide, thick belt with a heavy brass buckle. 'Come here', he said.

The boy, biting his lower lip so as to keep back the tears, advanced, and the man raised his arm. The woman, motionless until that moment, leapt forward and seized it. Her husband, finding strength in his blind rage, pushed her aside easily. He brought the belt down on the boy's back. He beat him unmercifully about the body and legs. The boy sank to the floor, but did not cry out.

When the man had spent himself, he put on the belt and

pulled the boy to his feet.

'Now you'll get off to bed,' he said.

'The lad wants some food,' said the woman.

'He'll go to bed. Go and wash yourself.'

Without a word the boy went into the scullery and washed his hands and face. When he had done this he went straight upstairs.

The man sat down at the table, ate some bread and butter and drank two cups of tea. The woman ate nothing. She sat opposite him, never taking her eyes from his face, looking with hatred at him. Just as before, he took no notice of her, ignored her, behaved as if she were not there at all.

When he had finished the meal he went out.

Immediately he had shut the door the woman jumped to her feet and ran upstairs to the boy's room.

He was sobbing bitterly, his face buried in the pillow. She sat on the edge of the bed and put her arms about him, pressed him close to her breast, ran her fingers through his disordered hair, whispered endearments, consoling him. He let her do this, finding comfort in her caresses, relief in his own tears.

After a while his weeping ceased. He raised his head and smiled at her, his wet eyes bright. Then he put his hand under the pillow and withdrew a small dirty envelope.

'Here's the money,' he whispered.

She took the envelope and opened it and pulled out a long strip of paper with some figures on it—a ten shilling note and a sixpence.

The Hands of the Blacks

I don't remember now how we got onto the subject, but one day Teacher said that the palms of the black's hands were much lighter than the rest of their bodies because only a few centuries ago they walked around on all fours, like wild animals, so their palms weren't exposed to the sun, which made the rest of their bodies darker and darker. I thought of this when Father Christiano told us after catechism that we were absolutely hopeless, and that even the blacks were better than us, and he went back to this thing about their hands being lighter, and said it was like that because they always went about with their hands folded together, praying in secret. I thought this was so funny, this thing of the black's hands being lighter, that you should just see me now—I don't let go of anyone, whoever they are, until they tell me why they think that the palms of the black's hands are lighter. Dona Dores, for instance, told me that God made their hands lighter like that so they wouldn't dirty the food they made for their masters, or anything else they were ordered to do that had to be kept quite clean.

Senhor Antunes, the Coca Cola man, who only comes to the village now and again when all the Cokes in the cantinas have been sold, said to me that everything I had been told was a lot of baloney. Of course I don't know if it was really, but he assured me it was. After I said yes, all right, it was baloney, then he told me what he knew about this thing of the black's hands. It was like this:—'Long ago, many years ago, God, Our Lord Jesus Christ, the Virgin Mary, St Peter, many other saints, all the angels that were in Heaven then, and some of the people who have died and gone to Heaven—they all had a meeting and decided to make blacks. Do you know how? They got hold of some clay and pressed it into some second-hand moulds. And to bake the clay of the creatures they took them to the Heavenly kilns. Because they were in a hurry and there was no room next to the fire they hung them in the chimneys. Smoke, smoke, smoke—and there you have them, black as coals. And now do you want to know why their hands stayed white? Well, didn't they have to hold on while their clay baked?

When he had told me this Senhor Antunes and the other men who were around us were very pleased and they all burst out laughing. That very same day Senhor Frias called me after Senhor Antunes had gone away, and told me that everything I heard from them there had been just one big pack of lies. Really and truly, what he knew about the black's hands was right—that God finished making men and told them to bathe in a lake in Heaven. After bathing the people were nice and white. The blacks, well, they were made very early in the morning, and at this hour the water in the lake was very cold, so they only wet the palms of their hands and the soles of their feet before dressing and coming into the world.

But I read in a book that happened to mention it, that the blacks have their hands lighter like this because they spent their lives bent over, gathering the white cotton of Virginia and I don't know where else. Of course Dona Estefánia didn't agree when I told her this. According to her it's only because their hands became bleached with all that washing.

Well, I don't know what to think about all this, but the truth is that however calloused and cracked they may be, a black's hands are always lighter than all the rest of him. And that's that!

My mother is the only one who must be right about this question of a black's hands being lighter than the rest of his body. On the day that we were talking about it, us two, I was telling her what I already knew about the question, and she just couldn't stop laughing. What I thought was strange was that she didn't tell me at once what she thought about all this, and she only answered me when she was sure that I wouldn't get tired of bothering her about it. And even then she was crying and clutching herself around the stomach like someone who had laughed so much that it was quite unbearable. What she said was more or less this:

'God made blacks because they had to be. They had to be, my son. He thought they really had to be....Afterwards he regretted having made them because the other men laughed at them and took them off to their homes and put them to serve like slaves or not much better. But because he couldn't make them all be white, for those who were used to seeing them black would complain, He made it so that the palms of their hands would be exactly like the palms of the hands of other men. And do you know why that was? Of course you don't know, and it's not surprising, because many, many people don't know. Well, listen: it was to show that what men do is only the work of men...That what men do is done by hands that are the same—hands of people who, if they had any sense, would know that before everything else they are men. He must have been thinking of this when He made the hands of the blacks be the same as the hands of those men who thank God they are not black!'

After telling me all this, my mother kissed my hands. As I ran off into the yard to play ball, I thought that I had never seen a person cry so much when nobody had hit them.

JOHN O'HARA

F*ree*

Mrs Ford tipped the bellboy and the porter, and thanked the assistant manager who had accompanied her to her room. They left, and she took off her hat and sailed it across the room, the first impulsive gesture she had allowed herself that morning. On the train, coming across the Jersey meadows, there had been a visible sparkle in the air, and in the station she had wanted to send her bags on with the redcaps so that she could go outside and walk to the hotel. There was always something about that first whiff of New York air, and it had looked especially good this morning. But there was an irregularity, and for a year there had been no such irregularities in her life, not even such a slight one. Then when she arrived at the hotel that slight irregularity had been followed by a major one: just as she was approaching the desk she had had an almost overwhelming impulse to register under a phony name. A name had come to her: Mrs James J. Jameson. It may have been a name that had been somewhere buried in her morning paper. It was a name that meant not a thing in the world to her, but for a second or two it had been a very real name—her own. But of course she had registered under her real name. There were so many reasons for that—in the first place, the simple one was that she had had reservations under her own name; the second, that the manager of the hotel knew her; the third—there didn't have to be a third, or a second, or a first. Not those kinds. The big thing was that overnight, almost literally overnight (three nights, actually) she had not been able to get away from the uninterrupted conventionality of a year.

Yet she was glad these impulses had been there. They showed thát something inside her was ready for this freedom that was hers once a year at this time. She sat down and kicked off her shoes and lit a cigarette. She put her feet up on the

119

small, uncomfortable-looking desk chair, and she leaned back, her right hand over her left breast. It was an attitude in which she often found herself when she was lost in thought, but now she was not lost in thought. She was just thinking that for three days she had not had to worry about how any-one else was sleeping or not sleeping. For more than three days she had not spoken to anyone she had not wanted to speak to, nor read anything she had not wanted to read. When mealtime came she had had to think only of her own wishes, and not the needs of her children and the tastes of her husband. There had been a telegram waiting for her downstairs, the same kind of telegram that had been sent two or three times to the train. She knew, to be sure, that her husband's secretary had sent the telegrams—maybe he hadn't, but it didn't really make much difference. The point was that he was all right and the boys were all right. Another point was that they all probably were enjoying her visit to New York as much as she was, albeit for different reasons.

She undressed and let herself into a warm tub, knowing that when she got out she would be cool again. The room was quite warm, but not so warm if you were naked. She lay naked and glowing on the bed, staring at the ceiling, and now she was quite cool. It was, indeed, a fact that her feet were defin-itely cold. It was a fact that did not disturb her much. She was thirty-three, and it was no news to her that her feet did get cold.

She began to plan her day. To begin with, she was going to spend a lot of money for things to clothe and adorn this now naked body, these cold feet, this head and hands. At the train in Pasadena Joe had suddenly been more generous than she had expected. He had given her all his cash (and he always car-ried a large sum), and besides what he had given her she had some of her own. This year she would buy one thing for even-ing that, if she wanted to, she could wear just one night in New York; something that would knock someone's eye out. It would be something that she would not dare wear in Pasadena. She would buy *that* dress *today*. The other things that could be sent home—they could be spread out over sev-eral days' shopping. She would have lunch alone and she

would walk a lot, and stop here and there to buy things that
cost five dollars, two dollars, a dollar. They might make Christmas presents (after all, that was what she was really here for),
but they wouldn't have to. Somewhere on Madison Avenue
she would be on her way from one shop to another, and she
would be feeling just fine, what with the air, a good lunch and
two cognacs afterward, and the whole feeling of being in New
York again. At the corner of—oh, say, Forty-ninth, traffic
would halt her at the curb. She would be standing there with
a dozen other peole, poor unconscious people who were
always in New York. They wouldn't know how good she was
feeling, so good that she would let it show in her eyes. And
then, on the other side of the stream of shiny black cars, would
be a man.

She would see him, but he would have seen her first. She
would know that someone was staring at her, and he would
have an honestly amused smile on his face, because he had
caught what was in her eyes. He would know. This man
would know.

She would look him straight in the eye, for just a second,
and then look away. But she would not be able to do anything
about what he saw in her eyes, and she would be flustered.
(What a word!) The cars would keep them apart, then the cop's
whistle would blow and the Madison Avenue bus would snort
and be off, and half way across the street she would come close
enough to touch the man and they would get as close to each
other as they could without touching. Not looking at each
other until they were so close. Then a quick look, and this time
he would not smile.

She would walk on, knowing that he had turned around in
the hope that she too would turn around. And would she? She
never had.

KATE CHOPIN

The Blind Man

A man carrying a small red box in one hand walked slowly down the street. His old straw hat and faded garments looked as if the rain had often beaten upon them, and the sun had as many times dried them upon his person. He was not old, but he seemed feeble; and he walked in the sun, along the blistering asphalt pavement. On the opposite side of the street there were trees that threw a thick and pleasant shade: people were all walking on that side. But the man did not know, for he was blind, and moreover he was stupid.

In the red box were lead pencils, which he was endeavoring to sell. He carried no stick, but guided himself by trailing his foot along the stone copings or his hand along the iron railings. When he came to the steps of a house he would mount them. Sometimes, after reaching the door with great difficulty, he could not find the electric button, whereupon he would patiently descend and go his way. Some of the iron gates were locked, their owners being away for the summer, and he would consume much time striving to open them, which made little difference, as he had all the time there was at his disposal.

At times he succeeded in finding the electric button: but the man or maid who answered the bell needed no pencil, nor could they be induced to disturb the mistress of the house about so small a thing.

The man had been out long and had walked far, but had sold nothing. That morning some one who had finally grown tired of having him hanging around had equipped him with this box of pencils, and sent him out to make his living. Hunger, with sharp fangs, was gnawing at his stomach and a consuming thirst parched his mouth and tortured him. The sun was broiling. He wore too much clothing—a vest and coat over his shirt. He might have removed these and carried them on his arm or thrown them away; but he did not think of it. A kind woman who saw him from an upper window felt sorry for him, and wished that he would cross over into the shade.

The man drifted into a side street, where there was a group of noisy, excited children at play. The colour of the box which he carried attracted them and they wanted to know what was in it. One of them attempted to take it away from him. With the instinct to protect his own and his only means of sustenance, he resisted, shouted at the children and called them names. A policeman coming round the corner and seeing that he was the centre of a disturbance, jerked him violently around by the collar; but upon perceiving that he was blind, considerably refrained from clubbing him and sent him on his way. He walked on in the sun.

During his aimless rambling he turned into a street where there were monster electric cars thundering up and down, clanging wild bells and literally shaking the ground beneath his feet with their terrific impetus. He started to cross the street.

Then something happened—something horrible happened that made the women faint and the strongest men who saw it grow sick and dizzy. The motorman's lips were as grey as his face, and that was ashen grey; and he shook and staggered from the superhuman effort he had put forth to stop his car.

Where could the crowds have come from so suddenly, as if by magic? Boys on the run, men and women tearing up on their wheels to see the sickening sight: doctors dashing up in buggies as if directed by Providence.

And the horror grew when the multitude recognized in the dead and mangled figure one of the wealthiest, most useful and most influential men of the town, a man noted for his prudence and foresight. How could such a terrible fate have overtaken him? He was hastening from his business house, for he was late, to join his family, who were to start in an hour or two for their summer home on the Atlantic coast. In his hurry he did not perceive the other car coming from the opposite direction, and the common, harrowing thing was repeated.

The blind man did not know what the commotion was all about. He had crossed the street, and there he was, stumbling on in the sun, trailing his foot along the coping.

Homecoming

'Good to have you back, son,'
the old man said.
'Nice to be back.'
'You've had a rough time.'
The eyes clouded with
guilt. 'Hope you don't think
I let you down.'
The younger shook his head.
'You warned me, dad. But
it wasn't the nails.
It was the kiss.'

Roger Woddis

Deep Search

It was that time of year,
so again they gathered at the
same place. Smoothly they
moved through the water.
Everything was noted; vibrating
sounds, shadows, shapes,
anything that would give a clue.
They reached the far shore and
looked to their leader—
'There's definitely something up
there,' said Nessie.

Kenneth R Cox

Nemesis

They watched the old man
collect his pension, followed
him like twin hawks, closed on
him with practised skill.
Startled, the victim
fell clutching his attackers
who found themselves stumbling
backwards off the pavement
into heavy traffic.
The Coroner said 'Accidental
Death.' The old man, once a
Commando, knew better.

John Johns

A Moment's Reflection

George stopped dead
A black car sped towards him.
It didn't stop; it didn't see him.
What to do? George never
could move very fast; no need
to since Milly died.
The car hurtled towards him.
Why make the effort?
Brakes screeched . . .
Wonder where she is now?
George stopped, dead.

David Taylor
Age 15

Different values, or, who got the best of the bargain?

Harris boasts he gave an
African a cheap watch
for an uncut diamond.
Sold it and gambled the
proceeds for more.

Abukali tells of the tiktik he
swapped for a wife
and two goats.
Harris chases further millions.
Abukali sleeps in the shade
while his children tend
his twenty goats.

R S Ferm

The Tunnel

The British burrowed from the
North, the French from the
South. They met beneath the
Channel and the necessary final
adjustment was really quite
small. Unfortunately, the
additional stress it caused was
critical and the party everyone
was having in the middle to
celebrate its construction was a
complete washout.

Charles Hope

The Interrogation

'What's your occupation?'
'I am a teacher.'
'Whom and what do you teach?'
'I teach people to shoot.'
Mental note—may be useful.
'Next.'
'What's your occupation?'
'I educate people.'
Another bloody intellectual.
'What's the difference?'
'I show them where to point
the gun.'
Dangerous.
The guards took him away.

D Wilby

Origins

The weary sculptor
wiped his brow. He had
toiled for many days, placing
a green mountain here and a
sparkling river there.
Lovingly he had moulded earth
into bone and inflated
lifeless lungs. Finally
he sprayed on feelings of
love, patience and joy.
His hands slipped
when he added hate.

Helen Brimacombe
Age 11

Follow On

GENERAL ACTIVITIES

BeforeReading

● Read an extract, poem, play or short story which:
— takes up similar themes or issues
— presents characters/settings in similar/contrasting ways
— is written in a similar/contrasting style or genre.

● Take some general issues or questions raised in the story and discuss them in advance to find out how much you and others know and what opinions you hold. After reading the story, discuss how far your ideas and opinions may have changed.

● Use the titles and/or the first few paragraphs to speculate and predict what the story may be about.

● Take some quotations from the story and speculate how the story will develop.

During Reading

● Stop at various points during reading, and review what has happened so far, then predict what might happen next or how the story may develop.

● Stop at various points and discuss why writers have made certain decisions and what alternatives were open to them.

● Decide who is telling or speaking the story.

● Look out for important quotations that help reveal the meaning of the story.

● Make notes and observations on plot, character, relationships between characters, style and the way the narrative works.

● Consider the various issues, themes or questions relating to the story which you discussed before reading.

● Build up a visual picture of the setting in order to work out its significance in the story or to represent it as a diagram. Devise a time chart, if appropriate.

After Reading

● Discuss a number of statements about the story and decide which best conveys what the story is about.

● Prepare a dramatic reading of parts of the text.

● Use the story as a stimulus for personal and imaginative writing:
— writing stories/plays/poems on a similar theme
— writing stories/plays/poems in a similar style, genre or with a similar structure.

● Discuss and write imaginative reconstructions or extensions of the text:
— rewriting the story from another character's point of view
— writing a scene which occurs before the story begins
— continuing beyond the end of the story
— writing an alternative ending
— changing the narrative from the first to the third-person and vice-versa
— experimenting with style and form
— picking a point in the story where the action takes a turn in direction and rewriting the rest of the story in a different way.

● Represent some of the ideas, issues and themes in the story for a particular purpose and audience:
— enacting a public enquiry or tribunal
— conducting an interview for TV or radio
— writing a newspaper report or press release
— writing a letter to a specified peprson or organisatyion
— giving an eye-witness report.

● Select passages from the story for film or radio scripting; act out the rehearsed script for a live audience, audio or video taping.

● Write critically or discursively about the story, or comparing one or more stories, focusing on:
— the meaning of the title
— character, plot and structure
— style, tone, use of dialect, language
— build up of tension, use of climax, humour, pathos, etc
— endings
— themes and issues.

Ho for Happiness

Before Reading

● What for you are the ingredients of a good short story? Discuss ideas in groups and make a list.

During Reading

● Pause after the phrases, 'my daughter is waiting for us down below in the car to take us to lunch' (page 2), and after 'perhaps she would not want a grown-up stepdaughter' (page 3). In each case, predict which way the story will develop.

After Reading

● Reread the opening two paragraphs of the story. Discuss the author's views about short stories, comparing them with your own list.

● In what ways does Stephen Leacock involve the reader closely in this tale? Look for particular examples of language, for example, by beginning the story with a question.

● Rewrite the story turning the 'romance and happiness' into 'crime and wickedness'. Think of a title that matches the original one.

A Violent Tale

Before Reading

● What popular fables do you know? Make a list and discuss their plots and morals.

During Reading

● Pause after the phrase, 'obviously deeply moved by the music' (page 5). Predict the outcome of the third lion's entrance.

After Reading

● Is 'A Violent Tale' a 'proper' story or just a joke? What is the difference?

● In what ways is this a violent tale? Do you think that comedy and violence should be mixed, as they are, for example, in cartoons? Write your views on this subject.

● Make up an alternative ending to the story.

The Reticence of Lady Anne

Before Reading

● Look up the word 'reticence'. What do you think the story might be about?

During Reading

● Pause after the question, 'Aren't we being very silly?' (page 8). Write your own final paragraph.

After Reading

● Write a short character description of Lady Anne and Egbert. Look closely at the text to help you build up your picture.

● Why does the writer choose to use quite a few difficult and pompous words and phrases? What do these add to or take away from your reading?

● How does Saki create tension and build up anticipation? At what point in the story did you guess Lady Anne 'was not feeling unwell'?

Baby X

Before Reading

● Discuss in groups the ways in which, both at home and at school, boys and girls are treated differently and the same. If you were writing a story about sex stereotyping, what ingredients would you include?

During Reading

● List all the made-up words in the story which play on the letter X.

After Reading

● Draw up two columns. In the left-hand one, note down all the sex stereotypes that are mentioned. In the right-hand one, list the examples where the sterotype is reversed by or for Baby X.

● How do your own experiences compare with those in the story? Does the writer exaggerate in order to put across his or her 'message'?

● What do you think of the concluding paragraph of the story? Write your own alternative version.

● 'Further Adventures of X and Y' — write this as a poem, play or short story.

The Objet d'Art

Before Reading

● What does the title mean to you? What associations do these words have which might lead you to predict what Chekhov is writing about?

● Find out a few biographical details on the writer Anton Chekhov.

During Reading

● What effect does the writer intend in using phrases like 'gentle reader' (page 16)?

● If you imagine that writing a short story is like neatly building a house of playing cards, make a note of how Chekhov constructs the comedy of this tale. Look closely at the text as you read.

After Reading

● What do we learn about people and their prejudices from this story? Do you think there is a serious 'moral' underneath the comedy?

● Act out and tape record your own version of the plot.

● Write your own story using the main ideas you have read about in 'The Objet d'Art'.

The Conjurer's Revenge

Before Reading

● This story has an unusual title—predict what the story might be about.

During Reading

● Pause after the words, 'It was passed to him' (page 21). Thinking about the title and what has already happened, write your own conclusion.

After Reading

● Act out or improvise 'The Conjurer's Revenge'. Tape your version.

● 'The Quick Man's Revenge'—write a short story, play or poem on this subject.

It's Slower By Lift

During Reading

● Look for ways in which the writer builds up the comic tension in the narrative. Make a list of particular phrases and incidents which you find amusing.

After Reading

● Do you find the events unbelievable? As this is comic writing does it matter whether the lift could have behaved so amazingly? What is the story saying about people and their habits?

● Write a short story based on a day-in-the-life of the Hall Porter. Try to use some of the techniques of comedy writing that TF Daveney employs.

A Touch of Genius

During Reading

● Make a list of the words and phrases which describe Danny's character.

● Pause after the words, ' "If I don't", said Danny, "I'll have a damn good try" ' (page 27). Write your own account of how he gets a pint.

After Reading

● Write a short character description of Danny which highlights his charm.

● Retell the story from Danny's viewpoint.

● Write another scene in which Danny charms someone into buying him a drink—this could be written as prose or dramascript.

An Assault on Santa Claus

Before Reading

● What do you predict this unlikely sounding story might be about? Look up the origin of the name Santa Claus.

During Reading

● Note down the *dialect* features of Timothy Callendar's style of writing. How would you write them in either your own local dialect or in Standard English?

● Stop reading after the sentences 'The door was swinging open. Barry's heart raced' (page 32). Predict how the story might end, bearing in mind what we have learned about Barry's character.

After Reading

● Rewrite this story using the first-person narrative 'I' so that we see events from Barry's viewpoint. You could alter some of the emphasis to bring out or play down Barry's villainy.

EXTENDED ASSIGNMENTS: HUMOUR

Humour and comedy come in many different forms. It can be the storyteller who makes us smile quietly, the comedian who tells sick jokes, the slapstick clown, or the sharply observed situation comedy where we laugh with and at the characters.
● Which of these stories made you laugh, smile or groan? Write a short review of the stories in this section in which you describe their *brand* of humour and your reaction to it.
● As well as telling a story, writers often want to make us think deeply about an idea, theme or issue. Is this true in these humorous tales? Make a short presentation to others in your group on the subject of 'Comedy Educates.'
● Mount a dramatised reading—complete with sound effects and music—of one of the stories in this section. This is best practised in small groups and then presented to a larger audience.
● 'In writing the short story it is the lines that are left out that are of paramount importance....The short story must depict more by implication than by statement, more by what is left out than left in. It ought, in fact, to resemble lace: strong but delicate, deviously woven yet full of light and air' (HE Bates). Write a critical review of three or four of the stories in this section with particular reference to HE Bates's commentary.
● Thinking carefully about these stories, what do they have in common? What conclusions do they lead you to in drawing out differences between a joke, a *very* short story and a short story. Draft out some notes on this subject and discuss ideas in groups. Now present a talk and tape record it.
● In good comic writing we laugh at the gap between how things *ought* to be and how they actually *are*. Write a critical commentary on three or four of the tales in this section, bringing into focus this point about good comedy.

Little Old Lady From Cricket Creek

Before Reading

● What expectations does Len Gray raise with the reader in this title?

● Think about an occasion when you met someone who later turned out to be very different from what you had first expected. What are your thoughts looking back?

During Reading

● This tale has lots of interesting twists and turns. Pause after each of the following points and try to predict what will follow:
  'He grinned. "Wouldn't miss it for the world" ' (page 35)
  'He laughed. "I bet she raises a few eyebrows" ' (page 35)
  '"Conked. Knocked out. And guess who did it?" ' (page 36)
  '"She came from Cricket Creek. I wonder if there is a Cricket Creek?" ' (page 36).
  'I opened a can of beer and then walked into one of the bedrooms' (page 37).

After Reading

● Look back over the narrative; list any clues as to how it actually concludes.

● What does this story have to say about our prejudices based on age, appearance and the background of others? Write a discussion essay on this subject.

● Rewrite this tale as a dramascript, trying to capture its various 'keep-you-guessing' moments.

Reconstruction of an Event

During Reading

●Note down examples of repetition and contradiction in the narrative. Think about *why* these are important to the structure of the story.

After Reading

● What effect is gained with the inclusion of such phrases as 'Just what happens'; 'Enough with the reconstructed dialogue'; 'No tree, no embellishments, no opinions, no lies'? Write a short commentary on the writer's technique, highlighting in what ways the story's structure is unusual.

● What 'crimes' are committed in the course of the story?

● Write your own short story based on an actual event, using the same kind of narrative techniques as Glenda Adams. You will need to draft and redraft carefully.

The Case for the Defence

During Reading

● Note down ways in which Graham Greene carefully builds up the tension in his narrative.

● Pause after the sentence, 'That extraordinary day had an extraordinary end' (page 45). Write your own ending to the story.

● What is your answer to the story's final question?

After Reading

● Rewrite the story from Mrs Salmon's point of view, using the first-person narrative.

● Write a critical review of Greene's style of writing, highlighting how he structures the story. Remember Roald Dahl's observation that in the best short stories 'there is no time for the sun shining through the pine trees'.

● Imagine you are making a short television film of 'The Case for the Defence.' Thinking about camera angles and timing, discuss how you would film it in order to maximise moments of tension and drama.

Bird Talk

Before Reading

● What are your views on children's responsibilities to their parents? Do these change as parents grow into old age?

During Reading

● Note down any phrases which suggest how Miriam's attitude towards her father changes during the course of the narrative.

● Stop after the sentence, 'The doctor came quite quickly, and after a brief examination turned to Miriam' (page 51). Predict the story's closing paragraph.

After Reading

● What is your verdict on the story's title? Is it well chosen? Look back over the text and examine the way in which the bird's presence is significant at different points.

● Compare 'Bird Talk' with 'The Reticence of Lady Anne'. Should comedy and death be mixed together in fiction? The subject of euthanasia might be mentioned in your discussion.

● Rewrite this story as a series of entries in Miriam's diary. Remember to use the 'I' narrator.

The Scarlatti Tilt

After Reading

● Look up the composer Scarlatti and the type of music he wrote. Does this add to your appreciation of the tale?

● What is your verdict on this *very* short story? Thinking about 'Bird Talk', are comic irony and death mixed successfully here?

● Rewrite this story in the form of a mini-saga (see Section Six).

The Spirit of the Law

Before Reading

● What do you understand by the words the 'spirit' and the 'letter' of the law? In what way are they or should they be different? Think of some examples.

After Reading

● As an exercise in story-telling technique, rewrite 'The Spirit of the Law' without using any dialogue. Does this improve upon the original?

● Write your own short story or play based around the idea of the 'spirit' of the law.

The Old Flame

During Reading

● Pause after the words, '"British passports this way! Have your passports ready, please!"' (page 55). How will the story end? Think about any clues so far in the narrative.

After Reading

● Compare this story with 'Ho for Happiness'. Does it confirm the view at the beginning of Stephen Leacock's tale 'that all the really good short stories seem to contain so much sadness and suffering and to turn so much on crime and wickedness'? Discuss this subject and then write up your opinions in a short essay.

● Retell this story as an article in a newspaper under the headline 'Pickpocket's Revenge'. Remember to include the sorts of details that sell popular newspapers.

The Man With The Scar

During Reading

● Stop after the words, '"I loved her"' (page 60). How will the story develop?

After Reading

● Somerset Maugham saw the short story 'as a narrative of a single event, material or spiritual, to which by the elimination of everything that was not essential to its elucidation a dramatic unity could be given'. Write a critical commentary on 'The Man with the Scar' in the light of these words.

● In his autobiography Somerset Maugham wrote: 'I cannot bring myself to judge my fellows; I am content to observe them'. Where do your sympathies lie in this story? Do you admire any of the characters?

EXTENDED ASSIGNMENTS: CRIME

● Why do people behave the way they do? What causes them to take one line of action rather than another? What *motivates* the characters in this section's stories about crime? Working in groups, choose one of the stories. Then, take it in turns to play the part of one of the characters. Each character is placed in the witness-box and quizzed by the others as to why they behaved as they did in the story. You might start with 'Reconstruction of an Event'.

● 'Little Old Lady from Cricket Creek' uses the first-person 'I' narrator to tell the story, while 'The Old Flame' has a third-person narrator observing the action from the outside.

Writer Graham Swift has commented: 'I nearly always write in the first person, partly because I prefer the located, ground-level view this gives, but partly because the narrator is every bit as important to me as the narrative.' What seem to you the advantages and disadvantages of the different types of narrative standpoint.?

● 'A first reading makes you want to know what will happen; a second makes you understand why it happens; a third makes you think'. How true is this in your reading and re-reading of the crime stories?

● What are your reactions to the ways in which these stories end? Look closely at the concluding lines of each story. If you find the ending unsatisfactory, try re-writing—or acting out—an alternative one.

Examination Day

Before Reading

● Science fiction usually projects the reader into the future. Which stories or novels have you read which have left you with memorable ideas about possible future worlds? George Orwell's *1984* and Aldous Huxley's *Brave New World* are recommended reading on this subject.

● What are examinations for? Discuss this topic in groups and then write up your views in an essay.

During Reading

● Note any details which suggest the story is set in the future.

● Stop after the sentence, 'They entered the Government Educational Building fifteen minutes before the appointed hour' (page 63). How will the story develop, bearing in mind some of the clues already given?

● Pause after the words, 'It was almost four o'clock when the telephone rang' (page 64). Write the closing lines of the story.

After Reading

● What view of a future world is the writer trying to project here? Does it seem credible?

● Write your own science fiction story, based around the idea of a government controlling children's intelligence.

Nice and Hygienic

Before Reading

● What does the title suggest this science fiction story might be about? Predict some possible storylines in groups.

During Reading

● Note any details about the time span of the story.

● Pause after the words from Turk, '"It's another commission. Elimination. Clean and hygienic"' (page 69). How will the story end?

After Reading

● Did the conclusion of the story surprise you? Look back over the narrative to see if there are any clues as to its final outcome?

● Imagine someone from the future steps into your bedroom one evening. The person offers you a taste of the future. How far forward would you choose to go? Why?

● Write your own short story under the title 'Murder Incorporated'. Give it a futuristic setting.

The Fun They Had

Before Reading

● The title of this story suggests an element of nostalgia. In small groups, talk about any feelings of nostalgia you have for anything; it may be people, places or events.

● Do you think schools are the best way to educate young people? What does 'education' mean to you? Write a discussion essay on this topic.

After Reading

● What are your views on the kind of schooling that Isaac Asimov pictures for the future? Could it come true? Which subjects on the curriculum do you think will come to be more, or less, relevant in the future?

● Write your own story, starting with the words: 'And the teachers were people . . .'

Murderers Walk

Before Reading

● This story is based on a law which says that murderers are hanged for their crime. What are your views on capital punishment? Should a civilised society take life in a premeditated and official way?

● The story also distinguishes between 'justice' and 'law'. Discuss your understanding of these two. Write up your ideas in an essay.

During Reading

● Make notes on the careful structuring of the stories-within-the-story. Pause each time you read one of the headings and think about what might follow.

After Reading

● Which of the following would you say the story is *most* to do with?
(i) the law and its failings; (ii) justice that never fails; (iii) terror and fear; (iv) society's treatment of criminals; (v) hope against all odds; (vi) the imagination.
   Or would you say the focus is on something else? Discuss the story's central ideas in pairs and then as a whole group.

● Imagine a sequel of episodes to 'Murderers Walk'. Write this as a short story or a radio/dramascript.

● This story is written in the present tense. Explain the effect that the writer gains by using this tense. Compare it with other stories in the science fiction section.

EXTENDED ASSIGNMENTS: SCIENCE FICTION

● 'To be believable, a science fiction story needs a firm grounding in reality'. Which aspects of the stories in this section would you call 'realistic'? Write up your views.

● What are the common features of these four visions of the future and other worlds? To what extent are the writers trying to *warn* us about the future? Do they offer any signs of hope about the way our world is evolving? Write your own ideas about life in the early, middle and late Twenty-First Century.

● Rewrite one of the stories and introduce a couple of additional characters into the action. How might events have turned out if there had been someone to outsmart even Emily Fairwell in 'Nice and Hygienic'?

● Choose one of the characters in these stories. Write their biography, or imagine yourself to be that person and draft out an autobiography. Use the texts as your starting point — then develop the piece to make an extended assignment.

● 'Surprise is everything. During a lifetime of writing short stories I have tried to creep up on myself and take me unawares. It's not easy. My other self is always looking round to make sure he is not crept up on' (Ray Bradbury). Write a review of these four science fiction tales focusing on the way in which they offer 'surprise' to their characters.

● Science fiction writing expands and expands. New writers and new stories are constantly offering different views of the future. Research in your library into the subject of science fiction. Put together a short project on the range of future worlds dreamed up by contemporary and past sci-fi authors. The 'Further Reading' list on page 153 will get you started.

Christmas Meeting

Before Reading

● 'Christmas alone'—what images do these words conjure up for you? Discuss in pairs and then in groups your views on Christmas. Do you see it as a *religious* festival?

After Reading

● What elements of the 'classic' ghost tale does this story include?

Look carefully at the way the text is structured. Look at the descriptions of people.

● Rewrite this story using the third-person narrator and then compare your version with the original. What changes in tone and atmosphere do you notice?

● Write your own story, beginning with the words: 'It gives me an uncanny feeling, sitting alone in my room with my head full of ghosts....'

Jarley's

Before Reading

● Research Dylan Thomas's life and then write a short essay on it.

● This story is set in a travelling waxworks. Madame Tussauds in London is one of the most popular tourist attractions in the world. What attracts people to look at waxwork models?

During Reading

● Make a note of the various historical figures in the waxworks and find out who they were.

After Reading

● Why does Eleazar become a wax model himself? Does he choose freely or is there something sinister going on in the story?

● 'The man of wax is an unchanging, unprejudiced and unemotional observer of the human comedy'. What do you think Dylan Thomas meant with these words? Discuss and then write up your opinions on this quotation.

● Write a couple of further episodes in the life of the travelling waxworks. Imagine yourself being drawn into the ranks of the models!

Exit

Before Reading

● What do you understand by the words 'psychic phenomena'? Look up the words in a dictionary and discuss their implications in groups. What aspects of the para-normal do you believe in and why?

After Reading

● Imagine you were a third friend alongside Carter and Hawkins. Write your account of what happened.

● Write the article that is printed in the local newspaper following the disappearance of Carter. Remember that various theories would no doubt be put forward in a way that would engage the readers' interests and emotions. Make up an eye-catching headline.

● Debate the issue: This house believes in ghosts. Remember to have two speakers for and against the motion, and someone to chair the proceedings.

● Write your own radio or television script with the title 'Exit'.

Legend for a Painting

Before Reading

● What is a *legend*? What is a *myth*? Talk about these two words in groups and then write up your views in a short account. Mention how we use these words in today's society.

● Look up the following words before you read the story: symbiotic; curative; concupiscent; carnivores; tautology; somnolent; porphyry.

After Reading

● Draw two columns on a piece of paper. In the left-hand one list the things you would expect to find in a traditional story about a knight rescuing a princess. In the right-hand one list the events in this story which reverse traditional or stereotyped ideas.

● Why do you think Julia O'Faolain devised the narrative in the way that she has? Is there a 'message' in the text? Think about the title.

● Write your own short story or play in which you reverse the stereotypes to be found in a popular fairy story, myth or legend. Or you could create a small children's picture book in this style. Have a look at *The Paperbag Princess* by Robert N. Munsch (Hippo Books) if it is in your library. You will find it useful to reread the story 'Baby X' (page 91) for further ideas.

Drought

Before Reading

● What images are created for you with the word 'drought'? Are these images from books and newspapers or from your television screen?

After Reading

● In what ways is this story similar to and different from 'Legend for a Painting'? Why might it be called a story of the 'supernatural'?

● Write a short commentary on the style and ideas of 'Drought'.

● What do you understand by the closing lines of the tale? Try to explain the various references to *prejudice* between black and white people that appear in the text.

EXTENDED ASSIGNMENTS: SUPERNATURAL

● From your reading of these stories what would you identify as their common ingredients? Think about both their content and the style in which they are written. Make notes on each story, draft your answer and then write out an essay aiming for about 700 words.

● 'What so many short stories have in common is that they are saying, in one form or another: "Isn't it strange?" They are reminding us that life, even everyday life, is more peculiar, more mysterious than we often assume'. Using this comment from writer Graham Swift, write a critical appreciation of two or three of the stories in this section.

● Write your own short story or dramascript in which you bring together characters from these stories to meet one another. What might happen, for example, if Eleazar met up with Carter and Hawkins?

● Look up the word 'symbolism' in the dictionary. Talk about symbols and images in pairs and then in groups. Write a short review of 'Drought' and 'Legend for a Painting' focusing on the authors' use of symbolism.

● Imagine you have the opportunity to interview any of the characters in this section of stories for a magazine article that you are putting together on the topic of the Supernatural. What questions would you ask? What might their responses be? Write the interviews you have and then the finished article, complete with quotations and a commentary which includes your own opinions.

● Which do you feel is the most important element in each of these stories—plot, character or setting? Give reasons for your answers, with close reference to the texts.

Elethia

Before Reading

● Can you think of something that has happened to you—or about someone you have met—which has made a lasting impression on you? Share any thoughts you have with others in your group. What exactly was it about the encounter that makes you remember it?

During Reading

● Make a note of details describing the appearance, thoughts and actions of Uncle Albert.

During Reading

● Write a short pen-portrait of Uncle Albert.

● Why was he so significant in Elethia's life? What does Alice Walker mean when she concludes: 'And she was careful that, no matter how compelling the hype, Uncle Alberts, in her own mind, were not permitted to exist' (page 99)?

● Talk about the similarities in style and content between 'Elethia' and 'Drought'. Write a critical review in which you compare:
(i) settings; (ii) characters; (iii) writers' style   and   vocabulary;
(iv) imagery and symbols; (v) writers' sense of protest.

The Woman's Rose

Before Reading

● 'Beauty is in the eye of the beholder'. What do you understand by this phrase? Can you think of some examples where this holds true?

● Shakespeare described *jealousy* as 'the green-eyed monster which doth mock / The meat it feeds on' (*Othello*). What did he mean by this? What causes jealousy? Is it necessarily a bad thing?

During Reading

● Pause after the words, 'to arrange my old black scarf across my old black dress' (page 102). Bearing in mind the story thus far, write an appropriate concluding conversation between the two women.

After Reading

● Why does Olive Schreiner end the story by repeating the phrase 'Spring cannot fail us'?

● What would you say is the main focus of this story?
(i) memories of times past; (ii) the worship of beauty; (iii) men's fickleness; (iv) women's subservience to men; (v) love between women; (vi) the battle of the sexes.
  Or does it lie elsewhere? Discuss this issue in pairs and then in groups. You might compare Olive Schreiner's story 'Three Dreams In A Desert' in *Dreams and Resolutions* (Unwin Hyman English Series) for a further perspective on the author's attitudes towards women and men.

● Imagine the two women in the story did meet up again long after the events described in 'The Woman's Rose'. What might their memories be? Act out a conversation between them. Tape record it.

Milk

During Reading

● Note the way in which the narrative standpoint changes.

After Reading

● What effect is achieved by Elsa Joubert in changing narrators? Rewrite one of the sections from a different viewpoint and compare your version with the original.

● People *are* what they are, but writers of fiction load the dice. Where do your sympathies lie at the end of this story? What is your attitude towards the reporter?

● Write the article about Maria Margarida da Silva that might have appeared in the local newspaper under the headline 'Tragedy in the new country' (page 108).

The Kiss

During Reading

● Thinking about the tone and style of writing of Olive Schreiner, make notes on Kate Chopin's stylistic technique.

● Pause after the words, 'and he sought her out in a rare moment when she stood alone' (page 112). Act out the conversation that follows to round off the story. Think carefully about their characters as already established in the narrative, and their *manner* of speaking.

After Reading

● 'A person can't have everything in this world; and it was a little unreasonable of her to expect it' (page 112). Why does Kate Chopin end her tale in this way? Does she direct her readers' sympathies?

The Breadwinner

Before Reading

● What form do family quarrels take in your home? What subjects cause parents and children to argue?

After Reading

● Write a short description of each of the three main characters, using textual details to help you.

● Retell the events from the viewpoint of one of the characters, using the 'I' narrator.

● What do you think of the boy's actions? Can telling lies be justified? Write your own short story or play which centres on someone telling a lie for good reasons.

The Hands of the Blacks

Before Reading

● Read Jan Rabie's story 'Drought'. What are its main ideas? From the title of LB Honwana's tale what might you predict about its storyline?

After Reading

● Write a short review of the two stories 'Drought' and 'The Hands of the Blacks' contrasting their style and content.

● What does this story gain by using the first-person narrator? Recast the plot using a third-person narrator.

Free

Before Reading

● Many people dream of escaping from their day-to-day responsibilities and being 'free' for a period of time. What would your ideal way of 'being free' consist of? Where would you go? Talk about this idea in groups.

After Reading

● Why does John O'Hara end the story in the way he does? What are your feelings as the story finishes?

● Imagine Mrs Ford keeps a daily diary. Write her entries for the days described in 'Free'.

The Blind Man

Before Reading

● Have you ever imagined what it is like to be blind? Talk about this in your groups. What have you observed about blind people and the way they go about their everyday business?

During Reading

● Note how Kate Chopin structures the story. Look at the length of paragraphs. Study the vocabulary she chooses and her careful punctuation.

● Stop reading after the words, 'doctors dashing up in buggies as if directed by Providence' (page 123). Predict the closing paragraph.

After Reading

● Write a review comparing the content and style of the two Kate Chopin stories 'The Kiss' and 'The Blind Man'. What are their similarities and differences? Include a study of the vocabulary she employs.

EXTENDED ASSIGNMENTS : THE INDIVIDUAL

● What the stories in this section have in common is a strong central character, strength being measured in different ways. Which characters did you enjoy reading about or even identify with? Write your own story centering on one of these characters, or bring together characters from different stories.

● In addition to 'spinning a good yarn' many writers want to make us think deeply about an idea or theme or issue. Make a list of the various issues raised in this section. Which themes do the stories share? Have any of the stories made you rethink your opinions or beliefs?

● When people write fiction they often do so based on something they have seen or done themselves. Which of these stories seem to you in any way autobiographical? What clues do you look for? Is it possible to separate out fact and fiction.

● 'A short story succeeds when it has the aspect of *verisimilitude*— the appearance of being true'. Write a review of two or three of the stories in this section, concentrating on their *verisimilitude*. Use quotation to support your views.

● 'Short stories have much more in common with poetry than with novels. Partly that's because of their compactness, and the way in which they're so tightly controlled. And partly because they very often focus on a single place or moment in time'. (Linda Cookson). Look at some poems you are familiar with—do you agree with the above comment? Write a critical commentary on four of the section's stories in the light of Linda Cookson's statement.

Mini-Sagas

Mini-sagas owe their origin to a series of very popular competitions organised recently by the *Sunday Telegraph Magazine* and BBC Radio 4. Essentially, a mini-saga is a story of exactly fifty words, neither more nor less, though the title can be up to an additional fifteen words long. It is this exact length which distinguishes it from the other short stories in this collection.

Before Reading

● Looking at the titles, try to predict what each of the mini-sagas might be about. What sorts of clues do the titles give? When you have gone on to read the mini-sagas look back at the titles to see if you could improve them.

After Reading

● Reread each of the mini-sagas. Talk about them first in pairs and then in groups. Consider the following:
— how each mini-saga measures against the judges' comments above
— the opening and closing words
— the use of dialogue
— the use of figures of speech, for example metaphor
— the syntax
— the placing of nouns, adjectives and adverbs. (One judge wrote: 'With a limitation of fifty words, you shouldn't really find any adjectives. And if you put an adverb in, it is usually because you have chosen the wrong verb'.)
— the rhythm and/or rhyme.
What is your verdict? Which ones do you like best? Which ones make you 'want to know more'? Write up your findings in a critical review.

● Write your own mini-sagas on subjects of your choosing. They might be based on a real experience or on something you have seen or read. You will need to spend some time drafting, redrafting and sharing ideas with others. Try to make your title—remember you are allowed up to fifteen words—interesting and majestic in itself; it should also link effectively with the mini-saga.

● 'The short story is the most *memorable* form of fiction. It is memorable because it has to tell and ring in every line. It has to be as exact as a sonnet or a ballad. It is, in essence, 'poetic' in its impulse' (VS Pritchett). In what ways do the mini-sagas compare with the various short stories in *Shorties*? How are they different from poems you know—or *are* they any different? You could start by looking at 'The Scarlatti Tilt' or 'The Spirit of the Law' and some poems by Mike Rosen (eg. 'You Tell Me', Kestrel).

● Rewrite any of the short stories in this volume in the form of a mini-saga. A good start might be with 'Elethia' by Alice Walker or 'The Blind Man' by Kate Chopin.

● Research into and compile a short project on the topic of *sagas*. Look up the origin and meaning of the word in a dictionary. Make a list of the ancient sagas, myths and legends. Think about modern sagas in the shape of television soap operas or perhaps newspaper stories. Illustrate your work and then present it as a talk to others in your group.

F*urther Reading*

This section has been compiled with three aims in mind:
— to enable students to read other works by writers featured in this volume
— to enable students to follow up certain themes, eg. science fiction
— to offer suggestions to students who are engaged in wider reading assignments for examinations at 16+
(All titles are novels or collections of short stories)

Humour

The Dry Pickwick, Stephen Leacock, Bodley Head; *The Penguin Complete Saki*, Penguin (1982); *Collected Short Stories*, James Plunkett, Poolbeg Press (1977); *It So Happen*, Timothy Callender, Christian Journals (1975); *Chekhov: The Early Stories*, Abacus (1984); *The History of Mr Polly*, H.G. Wells, Longman (1986); *The Stories of John Cheever*, Penguin (1982); *Kill-A-Louse Week*, Susan Gregory, Penguin (1986); *My Uncle Silas*, H.E. Bates, OUP (1984); *O. Henry Westerns*, Methuen (1961); *Feet and other Stories*, Jan Mark, Puffin (1984); *The Gold Bat and other stories*, P.G. Wodehouse, Penguin (1986); *Ways of Sunlight*, Sam Selvon, Longman (1985); *My Oedipus Complex*, Frank O'Connor, Penguin (1984).

Crime

Collected Short Stories, Graham Greene, Penguin (1986); *The Best Detective Stories of Cyril Hare*, Faber & Faber; *Collected Short Stories*, Somerset Maugham, Penguin; *Wives At War and other stories*, Flora Nwapa, Tana Press (1984); *Violence*, Festus Iyayi, Longman (1979); *Separate Tracks*, Jane Rogers, Fontana (1983); *Free from the Ashes*, ed. Kenzaburo Oe, Readers International (1985); *The Siege of Babylon*, Farrukh Dhondy, Macmillan (1978); *The Experience of Prison*, ed. David Ball, Longman Imprints (1977); *The Hottest Night of the Century*, Glenda Adams, Angus & Robertson (1979); *The Cone-Gatherers*, Robin Jenkins, Longman (1987); *Murder And Company*, ed. Harriet Ayres, Pandora (1988); *The Penguin Complete Adventures of Sherlock Holmes*, Arthur Conan Doyle, Penguin (1981); *Father Brown Stories*, G.K. Chesterton, Puffin (1987).

Science Fiction

The Illustrated Man, Ray Bradbury, Granada (1977); *To Sing Strange Songs*, Ray Bradbury, Wheaton (1979); *Earth is Room Enough*, Isaac Asimov, Doubleday (1957); *Science Fiction Stories*, ed. John L. Foster, Ward Lock (1975); *Paper Thin*, Philip First, Paladin (1986); *Galactic Warlord*, Douglas Hill, Gollancz (1979); *On The Flip Side*, Nicholas Fisk, Kestrel (1983); *The Early Asimov*, Volumes I, II, III, Granada (1973); *Other Edens*, ed. Evans & Holdstock, Unwin Hyman (1987); *Other Edens II*, ed. Evans & Holdstock, Unwin Hyman (1988); *Computer Crimes and Capes*, ed. Isaac Asimov, Penguin (1986); *Time Rope*, Robert Leeson, Longman (1986); *Fantasy Tales*, ed. Barbara Ireson, Beaver (1981).

Supernatural

The Collected Stories, Dylan Thomas, Dent (1984); *The Gods in Winter*, Patricia Miles, Hamish Hamilton (1978); *Daughters of Passion*, Julia O'Faolain, Penguin (1982); *The Penguin Book of Southern African Stories*, ed. Stephen Gray, Penguin (1985); *Strange Tales*, ed. Jean Russell, Magnet (1981); *Could It Be?*, ed. M. Marland, Longman (1978); *Sinister, Strange & Supernatural*, ed. Helen Hoke, Dent (1981); *Thrillers, Chillers & Killers*, ed. Helen Hoke, Dent (1979); *The Shadow-Cage and other tales of the supernatural*, Philippa Pearce, Kestrel (1977); *Twisters*, ed. S. Bowles, Fontana; *Dead of Night*, Peter Haining, Kimber; *A Touch of Chill*, Joan Aiken, Fontana; *Ghostly Companions*, Vivien Alcock, Fontana; *Tales of Natural and Unnatural Catastrophes*, Patricia Highsmith, Methuen (1988).

The Individual

You Can't Keep a Good Woman Down, Alice Walker, The Women's Press (1982); *Portraits*, Kate Chopin, The Women's Press (1979); *We Killed Mangy-Dog and other Mozambique stories*, L.B. Honwana, Heinemann (1969); *The Collected Stories of John O'Hara*, Pan (1986); *Debbie Go Home*, Alan Paton, Penguin (1965); *I Know Why the Caged Bird Sings*, Maya Angelou, Virago (1984); *The Sugar Factory*, Robert Carter, Angus & Robertson (1986); *Merle and other stories*, Paule Marshall, Virago (1985); *The Water's Edge*, Moy McCrory, Sheba (1985); *Bleeding Sinners*, Moy McCrory, Methuen (1988); *To School Through The Fields*, Alice Taylor, Brandon Books (1988); *After The Fountain*, Linda Cookson, Cassells (1988); *A Single Sensation*, Emma Cooke, Poolbeg Press (1981); *Sumitra's Story*, Rukshana Smith, Bodley Head (1982); *The Fifth Child*, Doris Lessing, Jonathan Cape (1988); *A Twist in the Tale*, Jeffrey Archer, Hodder & Stoughton (1988).

Acknowledgements

The editor and publishers are grateful to the following for permission to reproduce the short stories in this collection:

'Ho for Happiness' © the Estate of Stephen Leacock, The Bodley Head. First published in *The Bodley Head Leacock*. 'The Conjurer's Revenge' © the Estate of Stephen Leacock, The Bodley Head. First published in *Literary Lapses*. 'A Touch of Genius' ©James Plunkett: reprinted by permission of the Peters Fraser & Dunlop Group Ltd. First published in *Collected Stories*, Poolbeg Press. 'Reconstruction of an Event' © Glenda Adams, 1979. First published in *The Hottest Night Of The Century*, Angus & Robertson Publishers. 'The Case for the Defence' © Graham Greene: Laurence Pollinger Ltd. First published in *Collected Stories*, William Heinemann Ltd & The Bodley Head Ltd. 'Bird Talk' © Muriel Mell: reprinted by permission of The Spastics Society. 'The Old Flame' © Cyril Hare: reprinted by permission of A P Watt Ltd on behalf of the Revd C P Gordon Clark. 'The Man with the Scar' © Somerset Maugham: reprinted by permission of William Heinemann Limited. 'The Fun They Had' © Isaac Asimov, 1957: reprinted by permission of Doubleday, a division of Bantam, Doubleday, Dell Publishing Group, Inc. 'Christmas Meeting' © Rosemary Timperley: Harvey Unna & Stephen Durbridge Ltd. 'Jarley's' ©Dylan Thomas: reproduced by permission of David Higham Associates Ltd. First published in *The Collected Stories*, J M Dent. 'Exit' © Patricia Miles, 1988: reprinted with kind permission of Curtis Brown, London. 'Elethia' © Alice Walker: The Women's Press. First published in *You Can't Keep A Good Woman Down*. 'The Hands of the Blacks' © LB Honwana: reproduced by permission of Heinemann Educational Books Ltd. 'Homecoming' by Roger Woddis, 'Deep Search' by Kenneth R Cox, 'Nemesis' by John Johns, 'A Moment's Reflection' by David Taylor, 'Different Values, Or Who Got The Best Of The Bargain?' by R S Ferm, 'The Tunnel' by Charles Hope, 'The Interrogation' by D Wilby, and 'Origins' by Helen Brimacombe: from the book of *Mini-Sagas I & II*, published by Alan Sutton Publishing Ltd, Gloucester; copyright *Telegraph Sunday Magazine*.